ONLY DANCING

Why was I hesitating? What was the worst that could happen? That the magic clinging to that crazy, wonderful time would be lost? When Caroline visits the *David Bowie Is . . .* exhibition at the V&A Museum, she doesn't expect to be pitched headlong into a forty-year-old mystery surrounding her older cousin Jilly. But the bittersweet piecing together of old memories brings new insights — and unforeseen revelations about her old friend Mark . . .

Books by Jan Jones
in the Linford Romance Library:

FAIRLIGHTS
AN ORDINARY GIFT

JAN JONES

ONLY DANCING

Complete and Unabridged

LINFORD
Leicester

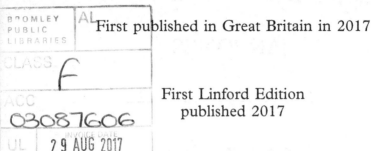
First published in Great Britain in 2017

First Linford Edition
published 2017

*A catalogue record for this book is available
from the British Library.*

ISBN 978–1–4448–3401–7

Published by
F. A. Thorpe (Publishing)
Anstey, Leicestershire

Set by Words & Graphics Ltd.
Anstey, Leicestershire
Printed and bound in Great Britain by
T. J. International Ltd., Padstow, Cornwall

This book is printed on acid-free paper

Acknowledgements

Any mistakes are my own, but I owe thanks to

David Bowie and all the musicians of the Seventies whose words and sounds and shapes and colours shaped my growing up years

The Roundhouse, just for being there exactly then

The Victoria & Albert Museum for staging the *David Bowie Is . . .* exhibition

Jane Dixon-Smith for another stunning cover for the Kindle edition of this book

My friends, as always, for the encouragement (and often the downright nagging)

and you, if I've forgotten to include you

Dedication

Only Dancing is dedicated to
Eve and Kay and Jane and Angela
and all our dreams of the future. I
hope you are living some of them
right now.

This book is also for David Bowie
and the music of the Seventies.
Wonderful sounds. Wonderful words.
Wonderful times.

Disclaimer

Only Dancing is a work of fiction.

David Bowie certainly played in all the concerts mentioned in this work — and I went to many of them — but any events and conversations involving him or relating to him are wholly the product of my own imagination.

The *David Bowie Is* . . . exhibition at the Victoria & Albert Museum took place in 2013. It was completely wonderful, but the three particular exhibits I mention in the story are my own invention, purely to facilitate the plot.

Jan Jones
September 2015

Author's note

When I wrote *Only Dancing*, David Bowie was a living legend. I wish he still was. Timeless and ageless, it never occurred to me that he might one day not be here. Except he is, of course. He is with all of us, the thread of his music in the blood, the nudge of creativity in the soul. Boogie on, David.

Jan Jones
January 2016

1

*1970. David Bowie played the Round-
house Spring Festival. I was there.
1972. The Bowie concert in the Royal
Festival Hall. I was there.
2013. The David Bowie Is . . . exhibition at the Victoria & Albert Museum. I
was here too, though I wasn't certain if
I wanted to be.*

Idiot, I told myself as I hesitated,
standing outside the museum in sunny,
everyday South Kensington, a lifetime
away from the new green girl I had been
in 1970. What was I worried about? I'd
visited the V&A countless thousands of
times for pleasure and for work. Today
would be no different. What was one
more exhibition here or there? What
was the worst that could happen?

Still I hesitated. *Out with it, Caroline.*
It was because it was *this* exhibition,

wasn't it? Was I really afraid that the magic still clinging to that wonderful, crazy, long-ago part of my memory would be lost?

As I wavered, there was movement by the doors. A porter emerged, carrying a stanchion, preparing to limit entry because the museum was busy. Not giving myself any more time to think, I ran up the steps and into the entrance hall.

★   ★   ★

Coming here was such a mistake. I knew it as soon as I pressed the button on the soundtrack headset and *Rebel Rebel* hit my ears. The immediacy of the song slammed into me. My forward progress faltered until I was hardly moving across the dark, compose-yourself antechamber. I'd have gone backwards if I could. Even this slowly, with people tutting and passing either side of me, before I was anything like composed enough I came out into the light of the exhibition proper and found myself, with an almighty physical shock, slap-bang in the early seventies.

I couldn't move. Bowie surrounded me, his face on the walls as beautiful as ever, his voice in my head, his art in my face. I was ricocheted back to those vibrant, colourful growing-up years, and I ached for my long-ago bachelor flat and that lost time when anything was possible.

Tears pricked my eyes. The magic hadn't gone, how could it? It shimmered in my past where it had always been, warm and vivid, threaded with excitement. With a fatalistic, teeth-jarring certainty, I knew that hadn't really been what I was dreading at all.

No, I was ashamed because the woman I was now didn't match the person I'd thought I would grow into. I'd hesitated outside the museum and dragged my feet in the anteroom, purely and simply because I hadn't wanted the knowledge forever in my head that I'd betrayed my teenage self.

My cousin Jilly was four years older than me, the late-born afterthought of Mum's eldest sister. Like many surprise children, she was doted on with awed wonder by her parents, winding them around her little finger from the day she was born. She was alternately guarded and indulged — and entirely misunderstood.

Jilly and I spent a lot of time together. Ours is that sort of family, by and large, but also I was the little sister she never had. In a household where she was the youngest, I was someone she could show off to, someone she could dress up and boss around. For cousins, we didn't look much alike. We had the same family-green eyes, but Jilly was tall and wild and beautiful with flame-coloured curls. I had a slight frame and straight dark hair. It made no difference. I adored her.

As a child, I shared her trampoline, her ballet lessons, her hated corned beef sandwiches (giving her my jam ones in exchange without protest). As we grew up, we rode the London Underground like a second home. We window-shopped all the boutiques along the King's Road and Carnaby Street. We spent whole afternoons trying on clothes. She made up my eyes with a Mary Quant kit I desperately wanted to own (though not, I have to say, as much as I later coveted her green zigzag Biba platforms). She took me to pubs and parties and told me things I didn't understand. And all to the constant soundtrack of records, auto-changing one after the other, after the other, after the other.

★　★　★

The first time I saw David Bowie play live, that Sunday at the Roundhouse in 1970, Jilly had made a tactical concession to parental concerns about her activities by taking me with her. 'Oh, you sillies. You never need to worry about me,' she said affectionately to Aunty Pam and Uncle Frank. 'I'm always all right. Yes, I know it's billed as the *Roundhouse Spring Festival*, but it's only music. And it begins at half-past three in the afternoon. What on earth happens at half-past three on a Sunday afternoon? Honestly, darlings, you don't want to go listening to people who have never been to these things themselves. Look, to prove how safe it is, I'll take Caro.'

Here, my parents intervened in a flurry of alarm. 'Jilly, dear, the posters say the concert goes on until eleven-thirty at night. Caroline has school on Monday.'

Jilly waved this away with the sunny nonchalance of someone who'd shaken the school dust off her feet for good last summer. 'We don't have to stay that late, and you know she'll have done all her homework by Saturday lunchtime. She always does. Don't worry, she'll love it.'

I did love it. I went to gigs with Jilly

many, many times afterwards, but they were nothing compared to that first mind-blowing experience. I was in the Roundhouse again now in my head as I stared at the poster facing me on the wall of the exhibition. It was from a later concert, but it was still David Bowie in all his magnificence. So much more untouchable and grand in costume and makeup and with the adrenalin running high than he was all the times I met him in person.

Back then, of course, I had no idea that everyone didn't go round to the dressing rooms after the show. That first time, the haze of patchouli and cigarette smoke, the patchy black paint on the walls and the air of faint dinginess only added to the magic as I tagged along behind Jilly, my head still exploding with music and lights and colour. We walked through the dressing-room door and Jilly was instantly swallowed up by her friends. I edged over to the side of the room where I could see a seat — only to find the singer next to me, quiet and reflective amongst the noisy crowd. And fell in love. Who wouldn't?

'Hello,' he said, turning his head as I tucked myself quietly onto a hard chair by the wall. 'Who are you?'

'Caroline,' I answered.

My eyes must still have been as wide as dinner plates, because he smiled slightly. 'First-time gig, yeah? Did you enjoy it?'

'Oh, yes,' I said on a rush of breath. 'The music and the lights and the words and . . . and you. I know your songs, and I heard you on the John Peel show two weeks ago, but this was . . . this was *wonderful*. It's so different. *I'm* so different now. I feel as if I've expanded inside. I've filled up all my spaces. I don't rattle around inside my body any more.'

He grinned, impishly, conspiratorially, just as if he was my age and not ten years older and a proper grown-up. 'Turns you on, doesn't it? It does me too.'

'Yes,' I said, with a sigh of pure pleasure that he understood. Because that's how I felt. As if I'd been flooded with life. Turned on.

We sat for a moment or two, isolated from the rest of the room. For years afterwards that would be my tranquil image, the place I thought myself to whenever I needed to take stock. A small bubble of perfection.

'How old are you, Caroline?'

'Fourteen.' It was what Jilly had told me to say. It would be true in a couple of months anyway. 'I came with Jilly.' I peered around the press of people and saw her by the door, the centre of a laughing group.

A relaxed look came over his face. 'Ah, yes, Jilly.'

'She's my cousin. She's pretty, isn't she?'

'She is.' He looked back at me and stretched to put his hand under my chin. 'But you — I like your look a lot. Good bones. Classic and simple. You can do something with that.' He reached absently for the festival programme I was clutching and started sketching. 'You need better clothes.'

I blushed. 'This is Jilly's dress. It's from *Bazaar*. I borrowed it to look right.'

'Dressing up only works if you can *be* the person inside the costume. Find your own style, Caroline. Shop the sales, get the best you can afford and never lose the music in your soul.' He stood, all in one sleek, unfolding movement. 'I'll see you around.' He dropped the programme back on my lap, plucked a tall woman away from the man she'd been talking to and left with her, just like that.

I looked down. He'd signed my programme and added a drawing of a grown-up me with a long bob, pencil skirt, nipped-in jacket, flamboyant scarf and heels. I had no idea how to achieve the look on my slender pocket money, but it didn't occur to me not to obey.

I thought about it all the way home. Great Aunt Dolly never threw anything away. I startled Mum and Dad by voluntarily offering to go to tea with her. Actually, she was really interesting to talk to when there was no one else listening in and telling her I was too young for those sort of memories. I came away with a 1930s Chinese silk jacket in jade swirls and another in a to-die-for mulberry mosaic. I re-seamed my A-line black school skirt to make it straight, and when I saw David Bowie the following month at the *Atomic Sunrise Festival* he gave me a thumbs-up of approval. That sealed it. Leaving aside the improbably long legs, it's a look that has served me very well for decades now.

⋆   ⋆   ⋆

Such a long time ago, those years, but with the music insistent in my ears, they were suddenly vivid in my mind's eye. I came back to the present only tenuously as I moved slowly along the exhibition, reading about David Bowie's early life and correlating what I read with what I remembered.

Here were the Roundhouse years.

The Hype, that was the name of his band then. I'd forgotten. And there was a photo of a gig, everyone absurdly young, and . . .

Oh . . .

My heart thumped. I stopped so abruptly someone bumped into me from behind. 'Sorry,' I murmured, sidestepping to get closer to the photo. It was focused on the band, but there were people to one side listening.

One of them was Jilly. Tumbling hair, hot pants and a long, sleeveless, crocheted waistcoat, it was impossible to mistake her. The ache inside me intensified, the past close enough to touch. What happens to us when we get old, to make all the lost years so painful? *Oh, Jilly, I miss you so much.*

It should have been no surprise, really, to find my cousin on any pictorial record of any London band in the early seventies. It was her milieu — and she was very photogenic. Cameras adored her.

What made this photo different was that Jilly wasn't simply listening to the music. Her body language said she was arguing as well. I shifted my gaze to the person next to her and received a second jolt. She was arguing with Blake! My husband Blake, much younger; before I knew him properly, before I married him.

I looked more closely. He'd changed very little over the years. Badged in the upwardly-mobile BBC uniform of a roll-neck sweater and slacks, he had the same controlled, lean form that he still had today. Even then, his hair showed signs of receding. Again, I don't know why it should have given me such a shock to see him in the photo. Blake was always one of the crowd, albeit older and better paid, and with the air — as with all writers, I think — of being an onlooker rather than a participant in the game.

No, what threw me now was that I hadn't realised he'd known Jilly well enough to have a row with her. It made me feel as though I'd missed a step in the dark.

I moved on, a tiny bit of unease

lodged in the back of my mind. *Stupid*, I told myself. It was over forty years ago. Nothing that far back should affect me today. It was the fault of the music, joining up my memories and making everything seem much closer.

The headset played Bowie's songs, snatches of interviews, audiences applauding. The exhibition brought my early life surging back. The *Life on Mars* tour, the concert at the Royal Festival Hall at the end of my O-levels, arguing for the whole of the previous two terms with my parents about not doing A-levels because I was just too restless and urgent and ready for life. Leaving school at the end of June and starting as a production secretary at the BBC with Jilly. Glimpsing the bands I saw regularly at the Roundhouse and the Hammersmith Odeon when they came in to appear on *Blue Peter* and *Top of the Pops* and the various chat shows. A manic, wonderful, crazy time.

Poleaxed by nostalgia, suddenly on the soundtrack I heard Jilly's voice emerge clear as clear from amidst a babble of street noise and background conversations.

'I'm only *dancing*!'

My heart stuttered. I couldn't believe it. Jilly! How many times had I heard her say that? *I'm only dancing*. To her parents, to her current boyfriend, to me when I didn't like the guy she was making out with on the dance floor. 'Silly,' she'd say with a throaty laugh, and she'd explain it to me again, tolerant and amused. 'It's only dancing, Caro. It's a contract, just for the length of the song. It's fun. It doesn't mean anything. Just dancing, that's all.'

I blinked away tears. Where had they got her voice from for the soundtrack? Had one of the parties been filmed or recorded and the tape been lying dusty in the archives all this time? Or was it someone else talking after all, and I'd been so meshed with the past that I'd mistaken her for Jilly? Either way, it didn't matter now. Jilly was long gone. Long gone.

I leant against the wall to regain my

equilibrium. I hadn't expected, when I was hesitating about coming in here, to be rocked by emotion over Jilly, but she was woven in and out of these years like fire. It stunned me now to remember how ever-present she'd been. How had I got so used to being without her, when at one time she coloured my entire life?

Stuff, I suppose. Children. Marriage. Making a living. When you are young, none of that matters ... but, insidiously, the world changes alongside you and responsibilities get in the way of self.

What about the colour and the laughter? Where did that go? Yes, everything I'd done had been rewarding; but 70s orange and party-pink had given way without me noticing to 80s magnolia and 90s beige, with only an occasional lilting touch of apricot to lift it. Somewhere along the way, I'd turned neutral. It was an appalling realisation.

Jilly had got me the job at the BBC. A production secretary, the same as she'd been when she'd started out. It wasn't as grand as it sounds. I was in the drama department, which meant a lot of typing of scripts, sending memos and organising coffee. I blessed Jilly for having pointed out the sense of taking office studies — specifically typing — at school during my pre-O-level year. Even so, I saw other people rushing around being busy in more exciting departments, and felt stuck in the slow lane.

'The important thing is getting in,' said Jilly. 'Keep an eye on the notice boards and apply for what you fancy from now on.'

But nothing did come up. My promotion to the happening end of the BBC came about in a different manner entirely.

I remember exactly why I was at the reception desk that day. I'd come down to see if a box of wigs that we'd been promised urgently was being sat on by

17

the porters. It was a quiet war, constantly waged, nobody ever knew why. Anyway, there I was, getting nowhere, when David Bowie arrived in the foyer with his entourage — and the day suddenly turned electric.

He had got massively more important since the Festival Hall concert, but I could see the importance was just another act, another layer. That was how he was. Every time he went out in public — even across the road to buy milk and cornflakes, probably — it was a performance he felt he owed to his fans. I loved him for it.

Now he leant across the counter and charmed the receptionist into directing him to the correct greenroom by the shortest route. Then he turned and saw me. Miraculously (to me at least), a real smile flashed across his face.

'Caroline. Love the clothes. What are you doing here?'

I beamed at him (yes, I know, but that was how he always affected me). 'I work here!' I said. 'I'm a production secretary. Jilly got me the job. Right now I'm chasing a box of wigs. That one there,' I added, pointing to a crate behind the counter with the name of a well-known firm branded across the top.

The receptionist expressed astonishment. 'So it is,' she trilled, and gave the box to me without a struggle.

David bent his mouth to my ear. 'Sounds dead boring to me,' he breathed. 'How about if I ask for you as my personal runner on the show tonight?'

I squeaked, even while my heart was thumping at the thought that he just might. 'You can't! There are rules and procedures. It would cause administrative chaos!'

He grinned impishly into my eyes. 'But would you do it?'

'Oh God, would I!'

He waved a hand. 'Take us to where I should be and I'll sort it.'

After which, I had precisely ten minutes to race back to the drama department clutching the box of wigs and tell them of my temporary secondment to Current Affairs. Where, and I say this with all modesty, I blossomed. Organising guests, sorting out cars, meeting people properly in reception, remembering all their little quirks and foibles for the dressing rooms . . . I was in my element. By the end of just that first evening, my old job was a thing of the past. By the end of the week I might have been working there forever.

★　★　★

Memories. Exciting, full of life, full of colour. Everything was coming back to me, that sharp wonder of finding something I was born for, something I could excel at. The blazing joy I'd felt at that particular discovery filled me again, lanced through with the bitter-sweet knowledge that without even realising it, I'd blown it.

I moved on through the exhibition,

knowing my brief co-existence with it was coming to an end. The rest would be David Bowie alone. *Life on Mars. Ziggy Stardust* and the Earls Court concert in 1973. Another at the Hammersmith Odeon — with Jilly ever more flamboyant — then 1974 and *Diamond Dogs* and David's departure for the States.

★   ★   ★

Jilly's departure too. To everyone's astonishment, she decided out of the blue in May that year to go globe-trotting. This time, my parents didn't let her take me with her.

'No?' she said to them. 'But Caro would love it. Travel is very mind-enhancing. Okay, tell you what, I don't want to lose my flat while I'm away. Caro can take it over for the year and look after it for me. That'll be better in any case for her than commuting from home to the BBC. It'll do her good to stand on her own two feet for a bit.'

My parents looked grave and doubtful. I looked sensible and attentive and crossed every finger I had behind my back. They said, oh, all right then, as it's a respectable block in a nice part of London. I expressed suitably humble gratitude. And when we were out of earshot, Jilly and I whooped aloud like nobody's business.

'Told you that'd do it,' said Jilly complacently. 'Nothing like presenting the oldies with a big bad threat to make them give in to a little one like lambs. Bring everything you've got with you, babe. Once away, you'll never want to return to the fold.'

I moved in the weekend before she left, helping her decide what to take and what to store. Unusually for Jilly, she hadn't wanted a big going-away party and a fuss, so it was just her and me.

'I can't believe you haven't packed yet,' I said, looking at the chaos in her bedroom.

'Too busy. Best way to be.' She

briskly folded two dresses, then picked up her green zigzag platforms.

I eyed them covetously. 'You're not really taking them, are you?'

She hesitated. 'Yes, I'd better.'

'But, Jilly, they're too small, you know they are. They'll warp your toes and give you blisters. I'll look after them for you.'

'I might need to sell them for food.'

'Sell them to me!'

'Caro, I can't. They were a gift.'

My eyes widened. 'Who do you know who gives you shoes from Biba?'

'Someone.' She looked again at the lack of space in her case, then thrust them at me. 'Go on then, you have them. Don't wear them at work though. You'll ruin them, all the racing around you do.' She grinned. 'I'm glad you're not in Drama any more.'

'Me too,' I said, putting the shoes on. They fitted perfectly.

'Skedaddle for ten minutes, can you? I need to make a private phone call.'

About the trip, I supposed. She knew

I didn't much like her friends Bob and Vanda. They were what Dad called dodgy and Mum described as 'away with the fairies'. Neither did I have much faith in their camper van.

'Are you sure the van will get you to the Mediterranean?' I asked later as we turned off the television and rinsed out our mugs of hot chocolate. 'It's all rust.'

'It'll get us somewhere.'

'Can *you* get you to the Med?' Jilly's geography was even worse than mine.

She grinned. 'It's the journey that counts, not the destination. If we end up in India, that's all right too.' She stopped teasing me. 'Don't worry, Caro, Bob will be navigating, not me. Listen, I'm off really early tomorrow. Night, honey. Live it up big time for me.'

'Ciao, Jilly,' I said, hugging her. 'I will.'

If I'd known it was the last time I'd ever see her, I'd have remembered every detail of that hug. As it was, I just let her go, thinking almost entirely of my own good fortune and the exciting prospects in store. Oh, Jilly.

* * *

I blew my nose and moved on. The exhibition was all about the States now. Everyone had gone and Britain was a greyer place. *Diamond Dogs* played on the headphones. I looked at the montage of Bowie's new life. Photos, designs . . .

Wait. Photos. One in particular.

I stared at it, rooted to the spot. It was unmistakeably Jilly. She was wearing a pink and purple paisley dress that I still had in the loft, and she'd thrown her head back to laugh, her tawny hair cascading across the arm of a man behind her. I don't suppose he'd have minded, they never did, but that wasn't the point.

New York studio party, said the caption. *1974*.

'That's wrong,' I said aloud. 'It has to be wrong.'

Because in 1974, Jilly had been driving through France with a bunch of pals on the first leg of her Mediterranean adventure.

Hadn't she?

2

I don't know how long I stared at the photo of the studio party. It was impossible. To my knowledge, Jilly had never been to America. Besides which, in May 1974, she had only just left Britain for France. She couldn't have been in New York — and yet there she was. After an aeon of just standing there staring with people passing around me, I finally pulled back to look at the other people in the photo. David Bowie was there of course, and I vaguely recognised several of the faces surrounding him in a last-seen-many-years-ago way. Then my heart really did stop, because there was one person I knew very well indeed. I went back outside in a semi-trance, sat on the sunshine-flooded steps, and dialled his number.

'Mark,' I said into my phone, my

voice sounding odd, 'are you doing anything special today?'

⋆　⋆　⋆

There had been a large, loose group of us working at the BBC back in the 1970s. All young, clever as paint, knowing the world was ours for the taking. Mark was a researcher on the current affairs team, about the same level as I was in production. In other words, we both raced around madly at other people's bidding, well aware that without us the programmes would never get made. Of the whole crowd, Mark was a proper friend. We smiled at the same things. We caught each other's eye and tried not to laugh if we happened to be in meetings together. We covered each other's back if one of us wanted to take an extra break or a longer lunch.

The BBC has always tended towards the hierarchical. In those days, with all the work done in-house, we had our place and were expected to keep to it. Mark and I were both happy enough on the bottom rungs of our respective ladders. We knew we'd move up when it was right and proper for us to do so, and that there was all the time in the world for it to happen.

Mark was different from the rest of us in that he was already married, though he was only a couple of years older than me. There had been a miscalculation with the girlfriend he'd grown up with (a sharp-featured, fair-haired girl called Jean who seemed resentful of us the few times she came to parties or to the pub), meaning they had to get married. Being Mark, being honourable, he'd done the right thing, even though he told me privately one slightly tipsy evening that he'd waited at the altar knowing they were both much too young. The point is, all the time I'd known Mark, he'd been off-limits, meaning we were free to be friends without sexual attraction getting in the way. It was such a comfortable thing you wouldn't believe. And I was young and in love with life and . . . ah, well.

★ ★ ★

'Hi Caro,' said Mark in my ear now, in response to my question. 'I was going over to the Bekonscot model village for *Lilliput Endings* today. Why do you ask?'

'How would you like to come to the V&A instead? There's something I want to show you.'

'If it's the models in the Architecture gallery, I've seen them.'

'It's not about work, Mark. It's something else.'

'Can we pretend it's about work for the expenses?'

Mark and I had our own company these days, him providing the research for independent film and TV companies while I managed the production projects. We'd combined bank loans many years ago to rent the ground floor of a converted warehouse in Camden Town, sharing a receptionist, kettle, fridge and photo-copier. Now we had the entire building and separate teams of staff, but still often worked together.

It's so funny how things turn out. Back when we started, the area was dirt cheap. Carnaby Street was the place to go, the place to be seen. It used to take Jilly and I a whole afternoon to get from one end of the road to the other. These days Carnaby Street was bland and boring and I could do it in under a minute. If you wanted hip, you came to Camden. Walking to and from the Tube, I was frequently transported back to the 1970s with its bright colours, the ethnic mix, the intense young things, the joy. Mark said it kept him young, working where we do. I tended to agree.

'We-e-e-ell,' I said now, 'there are some very nice architectural models on the fourth floor . . .'

'I'll be there in half an hour,' he said. 'Bekonscot can wait until tomorrow.'

I remained on the steps and saw him before he saw me, loping up Exhibition

Road with the semi-eager, long-legged stride that characterised him. He was nearly sixty now, but he didn't look it any more than I hoped I did, still the same Mark I'd met in my first week of work aged sixteen. Had I even noticed when his fair hair turned that rather attractive ash grey? It had happened gradually, his maturing face becoming a part of him, part of the fabric of my life. There had been just two or three years when we hadn't been friends and colleagues, and I'd been the poorer for them. I knew him better than I did my own husband. Certainly I laughed more in the office than I ever did at home. We'd celebrated the good times together and talked endlessly through the bad times, most recently when Jean announced she was leaving him after more than forty years of marriage. Mark had got quite remarkably drunk, raged about wasting half a lifetime, fallen asleep between one word and the next, and the following day had got on with life again, albeit with a hangover that had taken him the rest of the week to shift.

'Hi, Caro,' he said now, bending his head to kiss my cheek in greeting. 'What have you found?'

'*David Bowie Is* . . . ' I said. 'Have you seen it yet?'

'No, I . . . ' Like me, he hesitated.

I met his eyes. 'I know,' I replied. 'Come on.'

We flashed our V&A membership cards at the attendant and put our headsets on. I saw *Rebel, Rebel* hit him the same way it had me.

'Oh lord,' he muttered. 'Caro, I'm not sure I . . . '

'I know,' I said again, taking his arm.

We went around the start of the exhibition in a remembering silence. I pointed out Jilly in the early photo and asked Mark if he realised she'd known Blake.

He frowned. 'I don't think so. Not especially. People were just around, weren't they? He's never mentioned it to you?'

'Not really, no.'

We moved on. I watched his eyes widen when Jilly's voice appeared on the soundtrack. He agreed it sounded like her, but couldn't swear to it. 'It's a long time ago, Caro,' he said.

I stopped him when we reached the photograph of the 1974 New York studio party. 'There,' I said. 'There's Jilly again.'

'So she is,' said Mark, warily.

'And there's you,' I said.

There was a pause of half a heartbeat. 'Oh. Yes. I didn't recognise myself with so much hair.'

'Stop fishing. You look very nice. Mark, this photo was shot in 1974. What was Jilly doing in the States when she was supposed to be on her way to the Med with Bobby and Vanda?'

He expelled a long breath. 'I took her.'

⋆ ⋆ ⋆

'You took Jilly to the States?'

We were upstairs in the V&A

Members' room, side by side on a sofa, two pots of tea untouched in front of us.

'You took her?' I repeated. 'Why? And why have you never told me? You couldn't have done, Mark, I had postcards from her from France.'

'We weren't in New York for long. A couple of weeks at the most. She went to Europe as soon as we got back.'

'I don't understand.'

'It wasn't planned, Caro. Jilly was all set to drive to the Mediterranean with Bobby and Vanda's crowd, but they weren't ready and she said she needed to get away right then and there. She knew I was going over to New York to do that documentary on Bowie, the one that came to nothing. She came to me all strung up and tense and asked me to get her on the team, despite having resigned from the BBC. She said it was crucial she left the country straight away. She said we didn't have to pay her or anything, just get her on the strength and don't tell anyone.' He shrugged apologetically. 'All of us were fools for Jilly. You know that. I persuaded the director to let her join us as free production backup and off we went.'

I stared at him. 'She had to get away?' Even forty years on, I was enormously hurt that I hadn't known. 'Jilly told you she had to get away? She didn't say anything to me and I was with her the weekend she went! I hugged her goodnight and when I got up in the morning, she'd left. Away to the Med, as I thought. Why would she have to go that urgently? I could have waited a couple more weeks before moving in. And why ever wouldn't she have told me she was going to New York? Normally she'd be bursting with excitement at that.'

Mark gestured helplessly. 'I don't know, Caro. Maybe she didn't want you to know Bobby and Vanda were messing her about, because you'd made it clear you didn't approve of them and she didn't want to give you an I-told-you-so opportunity.'

I looked at him disbelievingly.

He massaged his temples. 'No, you're right, it was more than that but I don't know what. I got the impression it was to do with a man. I think she'd got herself into a situation and she was scared. At any rate, she was convincingly desperate about the need to disappear.'

Jilly could do convincing like no one's business, I knew that. And I also knew Mark had always had a thing for her that she would have exploited without question if she'd needed to. A kind of medieval chivalry. No words ever spoken, no possibility it would be requited or done anything about, just a steady flame borne for her.

I swallowed. 'Why didn't you tell me?'

Mark coloured. 'Ah.' He pulled a teapot across and poured our tea. 'She asked me not to. That was before we went. Then, when we got to New York, it was weird. The people around Bowie weren't being cooperative, despite all the preliminary work we'd done. They were welcoming in a vague, uncommitted way, but there was no structure. We got some rehearsal footage, some conversations — you couldn't call them interviews . . . '

I knew those situations. 'Infuriating,' I murmured, sympathetic despite the roaring worry inside me about why Jilly had acted so out of character.

He shrugged. 'It happens. Anyway, the director decided to cut our losses and pull the plug. He had something else in the pipeline, that fly-on-the-wall documentary on the cruise liner across the Atlantic, remember? He made a few phone calls and a week later we were on the *SS MoreMoneyThanSense* out of New York bound for London.'

I drank my tea slowly, filtering what he was saying, listening to the tone behind the words. Mark is my best friend. I've worked with him, on and off, for forty years. 'What are you not telling me?' I asked.

'Jilly didn't want to leave New York. She was . . . I don't know. She was in a strange state. Far too lively, jumpy as anything, and blanking it out by throwing herself into every distraction going.' He met my eyes. 'She scared me, Caro. If we'd left her there, I could see her in a couple of months as a statistic on the sidewalk, having thought she could fly out of the hotel window or something.'

I was dumbstruck and appalled. I hadn't known. Caught up in my glorious escape from home, I hadn't picked up on my favourite cousin's state of mind even though I'd shared that last weekend with her. How unutterably selfish I'd been.

Mark put his hand over mine. 'Don't blame yourself for not seeing it. She kept a tight lid on herself until we were actually in New York. When she let go, I was horrified.'

The roaring was even louder inside me now. 'How did you persuade her to leave?' I asked dully, feeling a failure.

He made a face. 'It's not pretty. The night before we sailed, I got her so drunk she passed out. I carted her to the ship, barely conscious, with the hangover from hell.'

'Oh, Mark.'

He made a helpless gesture. 'I couldn't think of a single other solution. She must have taken something on top of the booze because I had an appalling time with her. She would have injured herself flailing and raging if I hadn't hung on to her the whole of that first day at sea. Fortunately, everyone else was too seasick to do any filming, so they didn't notice. Once she sobered up and . . . and came down, she thanked me. She was subdued for a day or so, but then sort of clicked back into herself. She was fine making the documentary on board, rang up Vanda from Southampton and arranged to meet them at Portsmouth. That was it. I never saw her again.'

The thought hung between us. *Not until I brought her home in an urn two and a half years later.*

I cleared my throat. 'I still don't see

why you didn't tell me.'

He coloured again. 'She didn't want anyone to know she hadn't left as planned.'

As I said, I knew Mark. 'And?'

He shot a look of quiet desperation at me. 'If I'd told you some of it, I'd have had to tell you the lot. Caro, love, do think. She was strong-willed, disoriented, flushing God knows what out of her system and needed me to distract her. It was only that first day, and she made all the running. I was barely twenty, out of my experience, in a place I didn't know. And she was gorgeous, you know, even stoned and wild. I didn't want to resist.'

'Oh.' I was startled — and yet not startled. After all, I'd done something very similar myself later.

A dull red stained his face and neck. 'Precisely. I was really ashamed afterwards.'

Lovely upright Mark, always trying to do the right thing. 'I don't suppose she was,' I said.

He shook his head. 'No. It was just part of life to Jilly. There was never any question of anything more. She was older than me. I was married with a child and another on the way. Jean and Lydia were everyday reality. Jilly was a wild exotic dream. She used me and I . . . I let her.'

No, he couldn't have behaved differently, any more than I could have done in the days following Jilly's death. Those were the 1970s and both of us were too young to challenge the really big things in life. Standards were different then.

'Things once done, eh?' I said, squeezing his hand.

'Something like that. You want to see the rest of the exhibition now?'

'Go on, then. Why not.' We walked slowly through the beautiful glass gallery towards the stairs. I was finding it a struggle to process everything. 'I still can't believe Jilly didn't tell me she had problems. She never let a hint drop to you as to who she needed to get away from?'

'No, sorry.'

'It's weird. And then she just went to Europe as planned. Alessandro said she never did get as far as India.'

'Your tame Italian count?'

'Not mine. Jilly's. That's something else I've never understood. She sent postcards to me all the time. She wrote saying the van was rubbish. They spent more time repairing it than they did on the road. There are rest areas on the French motorways where you can camp for days without anyone moving you on, did you know? When they didn't have the money for the motorways and broke down in one of the villages instead, they'd have to pacify the locals until they'd earned enough to fix the engine and travel on. It was mostly Jilly who earned the money, according to her cards. What she *didn't* tell me was that the wretched van finally expired within sight of Alessandro's estate near the top of Lake Garda. He and Maria collected arty types. They both had inclinations that way and wanted to set up an artistic commune so they invited them all to turn the camper static and stay. Jilly made a bargain with Alessandro that she'd run the commune in exchange for board and lodging.'

Mark grinned. 'That sounds like her.'

'Absolutely. But not telling me about it really wasn't. She was enjoying the adventure, sending me postcards all down the west side of France (*this is such fun, Caro, and I'm sure I'll get used to the food soon! Don't tell anyone where I am, I don't want to have to come back to real life*), into Spain (*it's so hot here, you wouldn't believe it*), back up to France and along the Mediterranean coast (*dirty, crowded and overpriced — glad we're not staying*), then into Italy (*we can leave the camper on this side and get the ferry to Venice. Just think, Caro, Venice!*). The next card I got said they'd decided to take the plunge and head for India, so the cards would be thin on the ground, but she must have been at the Castello when she wrote it. She was still there months and months later when someone ran her off the road.'

And that was when my life changed. I'd had just over two years living the carefree bachelor-girl life in the flat. Some rebel I turned out to be.

★   ★   ★

The flat was on the fourth floor of Postern Court, a large intimidating Victorian building, situated in the hinterland where Russell Square turns into Bloomsbury. It looked extraordinarily respectable, thus proving that you really shouldn't judge by appearances.

The first day after Jilly left, her neighbour across the stairwell knocked on my door and asked to borrow the dining table. It was an arrangement they had. Fran borrowed Jilly's table and chairs when she had dinner guests, Jilly borrowed Fran's sofa when she threw parties. I helped Fran carry the table across, and she invited me to come back that evening as she was short of a woman. I got lots of invitations like that, mostly from people who'd forgotten Jilly was going away, or who'd never known in the first place. She had masses of friends. It was wonderful, even if some of them did call at the weirdest hours. To reassure Mum and Dad that I wasn't lonely, I told them about my third night when I'd come out of my bedroom in the morning to find an Aussie stranger asleep on the settee. Apparently, Jilly had given Hannah a key a couple of years back, with an open invitation to pop in anytime during her next European trip. The next thing I knew, Dad had turned up with his toolbox and a new Chubb lock for the flat door.

There were quite a few incidents like that. I smiled wryly now, thinking of one of them. I'd been in the flat two or three weeks when I heard scratching at the door early one morning. I assumed it was Fran running out of milk for her coffee again, so opened up cheerfully, only to find Blake standing there!

'Hi, I'm back,' he said. 'Why doesn't

my . . . ?' And then he took in that it was me, still damp from my bath, holding a towel precariously around me. His hand flashed down to his pocket. 'Caro, how nice. Staying with Jilly for a bit?'

We've laughed about it since, of course, but at the time I didn't really know Blake except from my original stint in the drama department. He was a writer in those days, just starting to branch out and direct things. He was pleasant enough, but he'd been to university and he went on climbing holidays several times a year with his college mountaineering club, which made him different. He was also older and cleverer than the rest of us. That made it even more embarrassing for me, stark naked under my towel, hair dripping onto the carpet, hankering after my first cup of tea of the day.

'Um, hi,' I said. 'I'm living here while Jilly's off travelling.'

Blake's mouth opened in sheer astonishment. 'She didn't mention that.' He stared at me again, then pulled himself together. 'I was going to offer her a lift in. I sometimes do if I'm over in this direction. How long is she away for?'

My eyes widened. I hadn't realised Jilly had *ever* gone into work this early in the morning. 'As long as it takes,' I answered. 'She's gone with a crowd. The idea is to drive across Europe. Maybe even go to India. It could be a year.' I smiled at him politely and clutched the towel tighter, wishing him gone.

He looked even more stunned. 'That's very sudden. I saw her just before I went on holiday and she didn't mention it.'

I shrugged, keeping the towel and my smile in place. It didn't do to annoy people above you in the BBC hierarchy. 'That's Jilly for you.' Her plans hadn't been *that* sudden, so evidently Blake wasn't in Jilly's inner circle.

'Well . . . ' He gave a brief smile. 'Do you want a lift? As I'm here?'

'No thanks. It's very kind, but I haven't had breakfast yet.' I didn't even offer him tea or coffee, just closed the door and collapsed in hysterical giggles on the floor at being seen in a bath towel by such a senior chap from work.

★ ★ ★

That was then and this is now, but some things never change. Blake still drives whenever possible, always preferring to be in control himself when travelling, rather than trusting to public transport. Even when he flies, he always hires a car at the other end.

These days, he and I cross distantly in the mornings, leaving each other polite notes and punctilious emails as to where we will be for the rest of the day. It wasn't how I'd expected marriage to be, but then nothing in my life has turned out how I'd expected. Not since the day I'd picked up the phone at work to hear Alessandro's voice telling me Jilly had been involved in a hit-and-run accident and I was required to come over to Italy immediately.

3

To this day I remember the feel of the telephone handset pressing into my palm. It was one of the new square plastic things, not the comfortable curved receiver I'd grown up with.

'Jilly's dead?' I repeated into it, uncomprehending.

'What?' said Mark, sitting bolt upright across the desk from me.

'We were all very shocked,' continued the sympathetic, velvet voice in my ear. 'I will send a car for you tomorrow. You have a passport, yes?'

'Yes,' I said, dazed. 'But I have work and . . . '

'You must take leave.'

'I don't understand. Who are you? Where is Jilly? What's happened?'

He told me he was Count Alessandro something *di* something, and Jilly had been working for him at the *Castello di* something else, which was his estate near the top of Lake Garda in Italy.

'But Jilly's in India,' I said.

My head whirled as he said no, she had been working for him in Italy, and I was named as her family contact, and Postern Court was still my address, yes, and the car would be outside my door at eight the next morning and to repeat this back to him, please.

I did so without retaining a single word. It was a good thing Mark was scribbling down everything I uttered.

'What happened?' he asked. He looked white and appalled.

I fumbled the receiver back on the cradle. 'Hit and run. I can't take it in. It can't be Jilly. Why would she be in Italy? He said she'd been working there. Why wouldn't I know?' Tears were running down my cheeks. I felt angry and empty, confused, aching and lost. I looked at my desk, wondering what I'd been about to do.

Mark came around to my side and hugged me awkwardly for comfort. 'Are you going to be okay?' He handed me a tissue to blot my face. 'I'd suggest nipping out for proper coffee, but we'll never get through the fans.'

I snapped back to my job in shock. That was it. That was what I was doing. David Bowie was flying in from West Germany for an interview. That was why Mark was here. He was the Bowie research expert.

'I'd nearly forgotten,' I said, horrified. 'I need to get down to reception. I'll have to leave a note for Personnel requesting compassionate leave for the rest of the week. There's no time for anything else. Oh, God, Mark, how can this be true?' I grabbed my clipboard and hurtled out, cramming my grief tightly inside me, concentrating on my task with every shred of willpower I possessed.

* * *

'You've drifted off somewhere.'

I blinked, focusing on today and the

stairs back down to the exhibition and Mark's piloting hand under my elbow. 'Sorry. I was remembering the day Alessandro phoned.'

He halted, turning a concerned face on me. 'Do you not want to do this? Is it going to bring it all back?'

I squeezed his arm. 'Too late, it's there already. No, I want to go on. It was David Bowie's show we were doing when we heard the news about Jilly. Do you remember?'

He glanced at me humorously. 'Caro, it's not a day I'm ever likely to forget.'

I felt myself blush, even after all these years, and was glad of the brief moment of dark before we restarted the exhibition.

* * *

In the event, the show had been easy. David Bowie was still the most charismatic guest we'd ever had. I don't remember now which album he was promoting, but I do remember that for one blessed hour, nothing existed except for him.

This wasn't everybody's opinion, of course. We had a new director, one who'd brought in his own presenter and who wanted to make his name with penetrating questions and hopefully a bit of a dust-up. Blow that for a game of soldiers. This was my idol we were talking about. To cover ourselves, Mark and I had devised a few awkward questions, but I'd typed them on a second page and carefully stuck it underneath the first with banana-y fingerprints. It would look like carelessness on my part, but the fact remained that a novice host wouldn't be able to ease the sheets apart, live on air, without looking clumsy. The questions on the top page — about Bowie's act, clothes, relationship with his fans and the inspiration behind the songs on this album — had been arranged to chime with his public persona. I knew he'd be able to speak on them for at least the hour allotted.

'For God's sake let's at least get some jostling fan footage,' snarled the director behind me as I led David off afterwards.

If our star guest heard, he didn't give any sign. 'How are you, Caroline?' he asked. 'We've barely spoken. And how is the beautiful Jilly? What's she up to these days?'

'I . . . she's dead.' I gave a great gasp, my perilous shield wall falling apart without warning.

We were passing a side corridor, giving on to a back staircase. The BBC is full of such places. In a flash, David whisked me around the corner and into the blind space behind the door. There was, almost instantly, the sound of speeding footsteps, a confusion of shouts, and then the thud of his entourage pelting down the stairs.

'I could kill for a cup of tea,' he remarked into the temporary silence.

I gulped. 'This way,' I said, knowing the quiet wouldn't last. Fortunately, it didn't have to. Just one floor up was a locked cubbyhole that I'd fitted out as an emergency kitchen for when guests wanted a hot drink and there wasn't time to get one from the canteen. The tiny room held kettle, mugs, tea, coffee, sugar, powdered milk and precious little else. We squeezed in. I flicked the kettle on.

'What happened?' he asked gently. 'Did she take something?'

I must have been in shock all afternoon, because it all tumbled out. How Jilly had gone travelling, it must be over two years ago now. How I'd thought she was in India, but I'd had a call today saying she'd been in a hit-and-run accident in Italy. How I was to go over there tomorrow. How I didn't understand and I didn't know what to do and how none of it made sense.

David made the tea and let me weep as we drank it. 'She was so vibrant, so bright,' he mused. 'So full of life. There'll be a reason for the way she acted. You'll find out when it's time.'

I blew my nose. 'Thanks. I'm sorry. Oh God, we'd better get you away. Where's your car?'

He smiled. 'Anywhere I want. The driver will find me. The front will be tricky, won't it? They'll have staked it out. Questions will be asked. Can we leave via the back?'

'Yes, there'll still be fans there.'

'All to the good. It's part of the fame. It's nice to thank them and it buoys me up.' He kissed me gently on the forehead. 'Let's boogie, girl.'

So I locked the door behind us and took him out the back of the BBC building where he joked and chatted with the dozen despairing teenage girls who'd suddenly had their faith in life restored.

When I went inside afterwards, however, all hell broke loose. Everyone was screamingly cross with me for having spirited our star guest out of the rear entrance.

'I've had his manager on the phone,' snarled the director. 'Bowie was supposed to meet his fans.'

'He did,' I said. 'He made their day. He talked to every girl clustered around that door and brushed his hand across theirs. Most of them said they'd never wash again. There was a duty cameraman out there. He'll have got the footage.'

'But you didn't tell anyone where you were going,' yelled the director, not mollified by this at all. He didn't want popular stars being nice to their fans. He wanted controversy.

That's when I lost it. 'My job is to make sure the programme runs smoothly and to look after the guests,' I screamed back. 'Which I did. And for your information, *sir*, my cousin has just died and I have to go to Italy tomorrow to identify her, and nothing you say at the moment — nothing at all — can even *begin* to compare with my grief over her.'

I dashed the tears away from my eyes, crammed things anyhow into my shoulder bag and headed for the door.

Halfway down the corridor, I heard

footsteps rapidly catching up with me.

'I'll see you home,' said Mark. 'I've rung Jean and told her I'm working late on a rush job.'

I stopped with a punch to my chest. The family. 'Oh God, I'll have to tell Mum. And Aunty Pam. How am I ever going to tell Aunty Pam?' I heard my voice rising hysterically.

Mark put his hand on my back and propelled me forward. 'Home and pack first. Eat something. Drink tea. Then you can ring.' He hesitated, a bit shame-faced. 'If your family is anything like mine, you'll only have to tell your mother and she'll do everyone else.'

'That's true.' I felt guilty at my cowardly relief. 'Thanks. Look, you don't have to come with me. I'll be okay.'

'If you could see yourself, you'd disagree.' He stopped a taxi, paid for it at the flat, stood over me while I packed, fed me food I didn't taste, set my alarm for ridiculous o'clock and made me drink tea. I rewarded him by bursting into tears again.

He pulled me to him. 'Oh Caro, hush.'

I didn't want to hush, I wanted to sob until my chest ached and my limbs turned to tears. So I did and he let me and when I awoke at midnight I was in his arms.

'Oh Mark,' I whispered, mortified.

He was already awake. He turned his head and kissed me. 'I know,' he said. His eyes linked with mine in the street-light coming in through the window. Twin tunnels of loss. Infinitely sad, infinitely loving. 'I'm so sorry, Caro. It's killing me to say this, but this didn't happen. It can't have done.'

'I know,' I replied. I was glad it was dark. Mark was my best friend and this felt the most right thing I'd ever done in my life. But he had Jean and their two little girls. He had commitments. We were honourable people. I touched his face. 'Don't worry. I've forgotten it already. Are you going to get into trouble for staying out?'

He gave a short laugh. 'And then some. She'll have bolted the door by now. I'll ring from work as soon as the switchboard opens and tell her I slept on the office floor. I had to do it once before.'

A tiny treacherous gladness warmed me that I didn't have to be alone tonight. 'Your front door's not the only thing to be bolted. The BBC will be too.' I turned to rest against his chest. 'You can leave when the alarm goes.'

He lay very still. 'Are you sure, Caro?'

'I'm sure.'

* * *

'We never have talked about that night,' I said now as Mark and I paused once again at the photo of Jilly arguing with Blake.

'Too precious,' said Mark simply.

I felt a jolt of pure surprise. 'You thought that too?' I said, looking up at him.

He smiled ruefully. 'Always have. We were so grown up, weren't we? So full of ideals and rightness. I didn't even dare tell you how lovely it was. What were we, early twenties?'

I nodded. 'Compared to today's kids, we were far more independent. Can you imagine letting any of your girls step on a plane to Italy, age twenty, to bring back their cousin's ashes?'

'God, no. But us . . . we all took serious decisions about the rest of our life as if it was second nature. It wouldn't have occurred to us to do otherwise.'

'Tell me about it.' I was silent for a moment, staring at the photo of Blake, thinking of all the decisions I'd made over the years for what had seemed at the time to be entirely the right reasons. 'I'm glad that night was precious for you too.'

'Let's just say it was a damn good thing I was taking the girls and Jean and her mother to Margate for the next fortnight. Out of sight, if not out of mind. As it was, when I came back . . .'

I sighed and finished his sentence. 'When you came back, everything in the whole world had changed.'

★　★　★

Italy was a confusion of people and noise and heat and red tape and just plain *strangeness*.

'Caro.' A man in his early thirties strode towards me across the Arrivals hall at Verona airport. His hair was flowing, he was wearing a billowing, full sleeved shirt, gathered at the wrists, and flared linen trousers. His hands were outstretched, his entire bearing expressed compassion. And yet . . . and yet I was folded into an air-embrace that left me lonelier and more confused than ever. There was nothing to Alessandro at all, just empty space and grandiloquent gestures. In contrast, Mark's warm, solid parting hug sat in my memory. I'd let it stay a little longer before making myself forget it.

'Ah, you have a look of Jilly,' said

Alessandro. 'I recognised you from her photos. So sad. We are devastated. Come, the car is outside.'

'Where is Jilly? What happened?'

He made a grief-stricken gesture. Jilly was in the morgue in town. We would call there on the way home. I must not expect too much. A car had hit her with some force and she had fallen from a great height. Recovering the body had not been easy. In short, there was little that was suitable to see for one so young and with such delicate sensibilities as myself.

I took his word for it. At the morgue they uncovered a tiny portion of Jilly's face and flame-coloured hair. My heart squeezed almost to nothing. I nodded painfully, signed where I was told to, turned blindly away. The cremation, Alessandro told me, would be that afternoon.

'So soon?' I protested, startled. 'But what about Jilly's family, my family? I need to ring them. They should be here.' There couldn't be no one from the family here. There just couldn't.

It was explained with many sweeping continental gestures that it had been several days already and there were regulations and I could take the ashes back for a remembrance service in England. This was the best way. Even had Alessandro found my details in Jilly's papers immediately, there would likely not have been time to arrange travel for all my family.

I was in severe shock, swept along too fast, surrounded by foreigners and a different culture. All that on top of a broken heart. I didn't have the ability to protest further. 'Jilly had papers?' I said, picking on the most ridiculous thing to be unsettled about.

Yes, naturally, because she was Alessandro's employee. Papers were necessary for the tax and the insurance. As well as being an artistic dilettante, it seemed Alessandro was a practising lawyer. Everything was in order, he said, and I was down as Jilly's next of kin.

That did startle me. 'Me? But what

about Auntie Pam and Uncle Frank?'

Alessandro shrugged. 'You are named. You are the executor of her will. We will go through the details over a cup of tea, yes? Jilly always preferred tea.'

The fight went out of me. I slumped in the car as limp as a rag doll. Outside the windows, the small town at the head of the lake was pretty enough, but I saw it through a haze of tears.

I wanted to howl, as I had last night. There was no Mark, though, to hold me close and fill the aching void left by Jilly. There was only this chilly dilettante with his pretend concern and the soul of a lawyer. I was too British to weep on *his* shoulder. Instead I roused myself to pass some inane comment on the garlands of flowers hanging from lamps and the corners of houses.

Another look of bright concern. 'Ah, yes, there was a *sagra* here, a local festival. Many tourists and visitors come for it. The tables are all pulled out, you understand, there is much eating and drinking and music and dancing. All was laughing and confusion. None of us can remember when Jilly went back. She was there, and then she wasn't. No one knows why. She must have decided to walk home early. It is a pleasant stroll, as you see.'

As he talked, the car had negotiated the last turns out of the town and was climbing a hill. With a sudden rush of nausea, I realised Alessandro was talking about the day Jilly had died.

'So this is . . . ' I clamped my hand across my mouth in horror, the sinuous loops of road now etched into my vision.

He gazed out of the window. 'Where the accident took place. Yes. A car must have come too fast around these bends and hit her. She was pushed off the edge. The car didn't stop.'

God in heaven, I was being driven along the exact same route that Jilly's killer had used. I screwed my eyes shut, my mind screaming. I couldn't have made any more conversation now if I'd tried.

'Are you all right?' asked Mark now.

'Not really.' I swallowed. 'I was remembering Italy. It was such a nightmare rush. First Jilly's poor, broken body in the morgue, then being casually told we were driving past the place where she'd died, and then — I don't think I ever told you this — then when we got there, they gave me her room to sleep in. Her room! Alessandro said he was sorry there was nowhere else prepared, but Jilly had run the house, so all was in confusion.'

'No!'

'Yes. I still feel sick, thinking about it. Alessandro indicated a couple of suitcases, presumably to pack her belongings into, put my case next to them, waved vaguely down the passage towards the bathroom, then went off to see about tea. I sat on the bed and howled.'

And I missed you. I missed you so much, Mark.

'How could there be no other bed-room?' said Mark, outraged. 'I thought you said this place was a castle?'

'Ah,' I said, and explained.

* * *

The *Castello Acqua di Fonte* lay to the north of Lake Garda. The medieval castle itself was a ruin. Alessandro and Maria lived in the sprawling eighteenth century farmhouse below it. It was, needless to say, unlike any farmhouse I'd ever seen in England. The car deposited us in a beaten earth court-yard and purred off to insinuate itself into an ex-barn, now a garage.

Once I realised what was required, I went round Jilly's room in a frozen trance, packing as fast as possible. I just wanted to get through the cremation and be out of there and back home again. I don't even remember doing it now. Instinct took over. Jilly had surprisingly little. Her ornaments went between layers of clothes, her makeup and writing case went in my own bag. I was still wondering why I'd been given two suitcases when Alessandro came back with tea to tell me we must go to the cremation in half an hour.

I cried all the way through it. Funerals should be grey and sombre and rain-swept. This was hot, sunny and Italian. In the background, people wailed noisily. There were children there, pent up, pushing each other. In a weird, back-to-front way it was like all our family gatherings in England, but they were what Jilly had wanted to escape from, so why had she remained here? Why hadn't she told us where she was? All these thoughts jostled restlessly in my mind. I still couldn't believe it was happening.

We came out into the heat, piled into cars, were driven back to the Castello. Alessandro, it seemed, did not lack for money. While people talked and squabbled and put tables together in the loggia outside, setting out glasses and plates for the funeral tea, I was ushered into the study. It was quiet in there, crowded with beams and heavy furniture. A rich square of carpet glowed in the centre of the stone flags.

Here was the will, Alessandro said, laying a crisp sheet of paper on the desk. Jilly had left everything to me. I must let him know my bank account so he could get her money transferred across.

I fumbled for my cheque book to give him the details.

There was a noise at the door. An elderly woman stood there with a toddler, one of the children from the service. I'd noticed his hair, because it was bright auburn, reminding me a little of Jilly's. I waited for the woman to talk to Alessandro and go away. She did so, gesticulating sharply, rattling her words like bullets. Then she nodded once at me and marched out of the door, leaving the boy in the study with us.

'This is Skye,' said Alessandro, getting out another sheaf of papers.

The little boy took a step towards me, attracted by the long leather fringes on my shoulder bag.

'Hello, Skye,' I said, giving him my finger to hold rather than the fringes. I looked at Alessandro. 'Is he one of yours?'

'I am his godfather,' he said, as if surprised he had to tell me. 'Skye is Jilly's son. Now he is yours.'

4

'I've never understood why Jilly didn't tell you or the family about Skye,' said Mark as we strolled thoughtfully back to South Kensington Tube station after the exhibition. Evidently, the reminder of the Davie Bowie years had set him recalling that time as well.

'Nor me,' I said. 'There was still a stigma attached to unmarried mothers, then, of course.'

'Tell me about it,' muttered Mark.

'Jilly would have paid very little attention to that, though. She'd have just breezed through it. Not telling the family was completely unlike her. I remember sitting in Alessandro's study in absolute, unutterable surprise as Skye stared at me with Jilly's eyes.'

'Your eyes too.'

'Family eyes, then. I gathered him onto my lap and cuddled him, and he didn't let go of my hand for the next month.'

Mark grinned. 'He's a good lad.'

'That *lad* is now thirty-eight and up for a prestigious architecture award.'

'Don't. Lydia's eldest is sitting her A-levels, for goodness sake. It doesn't seem two minutes since I was building sandcastles for Lydia herself at Margate.'

Yes, I thought. *I remember that too.*

★   ★   ★

In a daze, I signed everything Alessandro told me to sign and took Skye outside to where they were holding the Italian version of a wake for his mother. He sat trustingly in my lap at the long tables spread with food, helping me get through the evening just by the awareness of his small life within my arms.

Jilly's son. *Jilly's son.* It was almost too much to take in, except he was there, solid and warm, with a thicket of baby-fine hair and Jilly's eyes, making me feel in the weirdest of ways that she hadn't gone after all, that she'd left part of herself with me.

Which, of course, she had. I was Skye's guardian, but she had also stipulated in writing that no one, no one at all, was allowed to adopt him except me. In view of this, Alessandro had already had the adoption papers drawn up. This was why he had been so insistent on me coming out.

I was used to children. They were scattered throughout the family, underfoot at all gatherings. My brother had twins only a year older than Skye. I was a good aunt, I liked kids, I just hadn't ever expected to be looking after one full time this soon. Or ever, come to that. I was going to need help adjusting.

I left most of my food on the plate, balanced Skye on my hip and found Alessandro. 'I have to talk to my mother,' I said. 'May I phone, please?'

'What?' shrieked Mum, on first hearing the news. 'Oh my goodness.

Oh, the poor little scrap. Why ever didn't she tell us? Skye, did you say? Typical Jilly. Well, he'll be a comfort to Pam at any rate. Laura will take him, I should think.'

Laura was Jilly's older sister. I held Skye tighter. 'No, I have to look after him myself.'

My mother's voice took on a careful tone. 'Caroline, darling, I know you loved Jilly and you mean well, but you're only twenty and . . . '

'Mum, I *have* to. Jilly made me Skye's guardian. It's in her will. No one else can adopt him.'

'That's as may be, love, but . . . '

'Alessandro is his godfather and he's going to see it happens before I'm allowed to bring him home. Can you tell Aunty Pam, please?'

'Caroline, do you know what's involved in bringing up a child?'

'No,' I said on a half-laugh, half-sob, 'but you do and you'll only be a phone call away. I can't not do this, Mum.'

I swear I heard her mental cogs

engage and her backbone stiffen along eight hundred miles of telephone wire. 'Leave it to me, then. Let me know when you're flying back. Dad and I will pick you both up from the airport. I'll borrow one of your brother's car seats for Skye.'

★   ★   ★

Say what you like about my family — and Blake has since said plenty — when the chips are down, they rally round. By the time I'd landed — Skye still attached to me like a determined, auburn-haired limpet, Mum had gathered enough toddler gear to kit out a medium-sized orphanage and paid the first quarter's rent on a garden flat, two streets away from her.

'I know it'll be a longer commute for you,' she said, 'but you can't manage a toddler and a push-chair up four flights of stairs with no lift. It also means Skye can come here for the day while you're out.'

Like me, Mum was under no illusions about my need to work. Unfortunately, the Personnel department thought otherwise.

With hindsight, I was extraordinarily lucky that the day I went back to work (taking Skye as he still refused to be parted from me) was the one day Blake had come down to the BBC canteen mid-morning in search of a coffee. Normally he worked single-mindedly through until lunch, but he'd only recently returned from a climbing holiday and his body clock was still tuned to mountain schedules.

The first I knew of his arrival in the canteen was a sports jacket, crisp white shirt and tie halting inches in front of my face and his concerned voice above my head. 'Caro! What ever is the matter?'

I raised my eyes from the sodden mound of tissues next to my mug. I remember being surprised Blake had stopped, much less spoken to me. He generally spent breaks with his team, focused on the current project. He was gaining quite a name for himself in the drama department for edgy psychological productions. Yet here he was, pulling out a chair, barely glancing at Skye, just concentrating on me.

'I've been sacked,' I said, swallowing a sob.

He made a surprised noise. 'I find that difficult to believe. Why?'

'Because Personnel have loathed me ever since I moved out of Drama without applying for a transfer through the proper channels, my new director hates me, and I took unauthorised leave.'

'That last bit doesn't sound like you. There must have been a good reason.'

I gave an unhappy laugh. 'The best — or the worst, depending on how you look at it. I had to go to Italy because my cousin was killed in a hit and run accident. Jilly — do you remember her? She'd been living near Lake Garda.'

'*Living* there?' he said.

'She was managing a commune, of

all things.' I groped for another tissue. 'I had to identify her, and then there was the cremation, and then we had all Skye's paperwork to sort out. His godfather is a lawyer so he whizzed it through, but it still took an extra few days. I did ring here straight away to say I had been delayed. Apparently that doesn't count.' *And the rest of my team had clearly been told not to talk to me, and Mark was on holiday so I couldn't have a sympathetic tea and buttered bun with him and ask him what to do and all in all, I just couldn't cope.*

'I don't understand,' said Blake. 'What paperwork?'

'For Skye.' I stroked Jilly's son's hair as he nestled against me, staring at Blake with wide eyes. 'Jilly named me his guardian, but he was born out there, so the authorities needed something more official before I could bring him home. Fastest adoption on record.'

I knew why it had been so quick. Alessandro's driving motive had been the will. Jilly had stipulated that nobody else but me was allowed to adopt Skye. Therefore, once Skye was legally tied to me, his godfather's main duty would be discharged. I'd promised to send photos and update Alessandro with progress letters, but essentially that was it, done.

There was a moment of absolute silence. 'This is Jilly's son?' said Blake slowly. He sat back, his eyes resting on Skye. 'Well, that is a surprise. How old is he?'

'About eighteen months. He'll be two in February. I don't know how I'm going to manage with no job. I need to pay the rent and buy food. I can't depend on handouts from the family, it wouldn't be fair.' I rubbed my eyes and burst out, 'And we kept having to drive up and down the horrible road where Jilly died. It's right on the edge of a cliff. I can't stop thinking about it.'

'That's natural,' he said, patting my hand sympathetically, 'but she wouldn't have felt anything, falling from height onto that sort of terrain. It's tragic, Caro, but you have to concentrate on

Skye now. He's the important one.'

'Of course he is, and I will. That's why I need a job and a steady income. It's so unfair. Can I sue for wrongful dismissal, do you suppose?'

Blake stood up. 'Easily, but it won't come to that. Stay there. I'll be back.' He felt in his pocket for a handful of change. 'Here, get yourself another tea and a slice of cake.'

It seemed he really was making a name for himself. An hour later I was reinstated on full pay, albeit in a different department because the director refused to have me back, and with an apology to boot. I even had the rest of the week off to sort out my affairs. Personnel still hated me though, so when a few years later the bean counters started screaming about accountability and outsourcing, I was one of the first to be offered redundancy. By then I was married to Blake and we had Ellie as a little sister for Skye, so I took the money and stepped out into the scary world of independent production.

* ★ *

'Are you coming back to the office?' asked Mark as the Tube approached Camden Town.

I roused myself. We'd worked together so long we were comfortable travelling in silence, locked in our private thoughts. 'No, I'll go straight home. All those memories have taken it out of me. See you at Ellie's housewarming on Saturday.' I kissed his cheek.

'I'll be there,' he replied.

Blake had emailed that he was going to be late and might stay in town. This wasn't uncommon. To be honest, I rather liked having the house to myself. It had surprised me, considering the urgency with which Blake had wooed and wed me, how polite and unexciting marriage should afterwards turn out to be. Possibly it was because we'd never had a honeymoon period. There had been Skye right from the start, then Ellie, and also I'd always worked. Blake's income from writing and directing tended to be erratic, so my wages were necessary, but in any case I needed to work for *me*, not just to pay the bills. Work was where I came alive. At work I was the real me, the domestic version of me was just a pale imitation.

Not today, though. If I was going to wallow in old memories, I'd do it properly. Stirred by the David Bowie exhibition, I poured myself a glass of wine and got out Jilly's letters.

I had found them as soon as I'd packed her things up. Jilly's writing case in those days holding no secrets from me. Opening the near invisible zip on the inner cover, I'd been stunned to see nearly two years of thin airmail paper filled with her flamboyant handwriting. At the time I was too full of grief, and too overwhelmed by the challenge of suddenly becoming a single mum to a youngster who was also grieving for his mother, to do anything other than read greedily through and put them aside. Jilly didn't want anyone to know who Skye's father was. Jilly loved Skye and wanted me and no one else to look after him. Those were the important bits. I'd zipped the letters back inside the hidden flap and put the writing folder in a drawer. Now, I drew them out again.

Caro, I'm not writing this in clear because, well, just because. You know me, though, and I'm depending on that. About Skye — I love him to bits, but it wasn't planned. I was only dancing, the same as I think you'd like to do, except you're a better person than me. It really was only dancing, Caro. I never expected it would change my life. There are reasons why I'm not saying who Skye's father is. Trust me, though, he has the best of genes. He'll grow up a brilliant boy who will look after me beautifully in my old age. Caro, darling, I'm dying to talk to you, but I can't unless I let everyone know about Skye, and I really can't do that just yet. What I do want is for you to bring him up if anything happens to me. You, Caro. You and no one else. Not that I'm expecting any problems, but having a child makes you think about the future. Alessandro is shocked I haven't made a will yet. I've told him what I want — he'll see it happens. The Castello Acqua di Fonte isn't where I would have chosen to settle if I were a free agent, but the van breaking down here turned out to be a godsend. I'm sorry I've misled you about India, but when I tell you everything, you'll understand. When Skye's a bit older, he and I might take off again and go there anyway. Or perhaps I'll stick with commune life until he's five or six, then come home.

But she hadn't. Her bright future had been wiped out by a hit-and-run driver. Mine too. All the wondrous things I'd thought I'd have plenty of time to savour and grow into, all put aside for the reality of managing a young family on zero experience and not quite enough money.

A young family. Yes, that was the next

thunderbolt. Sometimes, everything really does come at once, doesn't it?

I can't blame myself for not noticing straight away. With my job assured, thanks to Blake, I threw myself into shifting everything out of Postern Court and into the new flat. By dint of talking non-stop to Skye and introducing him to the wide circle of family members Mum had recruited to help with the move, I managed to gradually ease him off me. This was liberating for both of us. He turned out to be a sociable boy. He liked the bustle of moving. He liked riding between the two flats in cars. He especially liked Blake's car because Blake had appropriated one of the donated child's car seats and fixed a toy steering wheel to the back of the passenger seat where Skye could reach it.

'I thought it would tempt him away from holding your hand the whole time,' he explained with a smile.

Blake. He was another reason I hadn't given a thought to myself and my monthly cycle. At first I assumed he was simply being solicitous out of an awkward feeling of responsibility for having been the one who found me weeping in the canteen and got my job back for me. But he kept on being helpful. I wasn't honestly sure what to make of him.

'New fella, Caroline?' said my brother on the sweltering day Blake joined in with manhandling all Jilly's furniture down four flights of stairs, into a hired van and out again at the new flat.

'No,' I said, flustered. 'He's just a friend.'

Richard made a disbelieving sound and exchanged a speaking glance with Dad. 'Come off it. Have you seen the way he looks at you and Skye?'

Incomprehensible though it was, Blake did genuinely seem to be interested in me. He mowed the grass at the new flat so I could take Skye outside. He blew up the paddling pool one of my cousins had passed down, mended the punctures and filled it with water so Skye could play in it. He even played with him, getting his nice clothes thoroughly soaked and not seeming to mind a bit.

He came to Jilly's memorial service. He made a point of meeting me for a mid-morning coffee on my first day back at work and asking how the Light Entertainment department was shaping up. He was there to drive me home.

'You could do worse,' said Mum elliptically. 'It's not every man who's willing to take on a child as well as a bride.'

'Mum, I don't even know him properly.'

'Whose fault is that? No one ever does to begin with. He's taken a shine to you and Skye. That's in his favour for a start.'

My head was too full of new things, that was the problem. I liked Blake, but I wasn't anywhere near ready for a relationship. I was still adapting to the hugeness of looking after Skye. I was striving to do well in the new job. And ever-present was the need to keep a lid on the immense cauldron of tears still sloshing around inside me about Jilly.

I hadn't had enough time or space to grieve. The misery pushed against my skin all the time, threatening to spill over. What I desperately wanted was someone to talk to, someone who would listen and sympathise and not judge. I was looking at the calendar, working out when Mark would get back from Margate, when it burst upon me in a moment of quite appalling realisation that there might be another reason I was feeling so tired and weepy.

* * *

Mark, I thought, staring at the result of the pregnancy test in stunned, frozen horror. *I have to see Mark*. Not that he could do anything, not that either of us could do anything, but he would have to know and I was frantic to talk everything through with him.

The internal phone, however, delivered a further bombshell. Mark had returned from Margate with mumps. Severe mumps. He would be off work for three or four weeks.

I put down the receiver, shaking with full-blown terror. I couldn't talk to Mark, I couldn't phone him, I couldn't write to him. Furthermore, I suddenly saw with awful clarity that as I had no boyfriend, even if I did nothing, people here were bound to suspect Mark of being the father. We had worked together, we often took lunch breaks together. Even though we were now in different departments, someone was bound to speculate. There would be whispers, gossip, rumours . . .

Oh God. Even more chilling was the thought that some sanctimonious person might suggest that '*there's probably nothing in it, but Jean ought to know*'.

Jean would be distraught. Mark would be devastated. His little girls . . .

I couldn't bring either of them — any of them — that pain.

That was the day Blake asked me out for a meal.

★ ★ ★

The decision, I told myself afterwards, was absolutely the right one. Blake was caring, flattering, eager, and he adored Skye. His arm slipping around my waist as we left the restaurant confirmed it. I didn't even have to make any of the running, I simply had to accept. Like the little tick-boxes you get on forms. 'Please untick the box if you do not want things to go any further with this man.' I didn't untick the box. Things went further. And in a great deal less than the fullness of time, there I was, standing in the registry office, signing my new name under his.

We didn't have a honeymoon. Blake thought it would be unsettling for Skye, and he was concerned that I needed to establish myself with my new production team before taking time off. He would give up one of his climbing fortnights and we could have a family holiday in the spring instead.

I agreed, not letting on by so much as a tremulous smile that I expected to be involved in a rather different kind of production come the spring.

* * *

It had been weeks since I'd said goodbye to Mark on that morning I'd gone to Italy. It was pure coincidence that I was at a canteen table in direct line of sight of the doorway on his first day back at work after the mumps. Our eyes met, he hesitated, and for several dozen heartbeats the Terrible Error klaxon went off full blast in my head.

This is what absence does. This is what panic does. This was why marriage to Blake hadn't cured my inner turmoil after all. The truth stunned me with its enormity. Oh dear God, how in heaven's name was I going to get through the next twenty minutes without letting Mark know?

'Hi,' said Mark, sitting down awkwardly with his tray. 'Long time no see. How have you been?'

'Um. Surviving,' I said. 'How are

you? Are you properly better now? You look terrible.'

He gave a shaky smile. 'Now I know I'm back. You couldn't just lie like everyone else and say how well I'm looking? Thank you, Caro, yes, I'm bored out of my skull, but I'm better.'

I grinned. 'Good. How was Margate?'

He rubbed his face. 'Margate was Margate. I spent most of it on the beach with the girls.'

There was a tiny silence, a gap waiting to be filled. I obliged. 'By yourself? What about Jean and her mother?'

He gave a soundless sigh. 'Jean was mostly throwing up.'

The sword thrust was unexpected, swift, and cleaved straight through my breastbone. Everything I might have said died right there on my lips. The tiny flicker of hope in my heart expired along with it. 'Not food poisoning, I take it?' I quipped bravely.

'No.'

So now he was even more committed. I managed a quite remarkably creditable smile under the circumstances. 'Congratulations.'

'Thanks.' He cleared his throat. 'I understand congratulations are in order for you too.'

For a moment my panic levels went soaring through the ceiling. *How could he know?* Then I saw his gaze resting on the shiny new ring on my left hand.

'Oh, that, yes. It was all a bit sudden, really. Did you hear about Italy? Has anyone said?'

His expression became properly Mark again. 'Oh lord, Caro. Jilly. I'd completely forgotten. Sorry. Was it horrible? I *was* thinking about you at the time.'

'Yes, it was horrible, but . . . ' I stopped and started again. 'The thing is, when I arrived, I was told Jilly had had a baby out there. She left him to my care.'

Mark's fork clattered to the plate. 'What?'

'His name is Skye. He's very . . . he's very sweet. He's got Jilly's hair. I've adopted him. So you see, when

Blake . . . ' I stopped again. 'As I say, it all happened a bit fast.'

Mark had only been toying with his food. Now he pushed it away. I'd already given up on mine.

'Caro . . . '

'Mark, I . . . '

We met each other's eyes. I don't know what he saw in mine, but his expression was a dead ringer for how the WW1 soldiers must have looked on being told they had to leave the trenches and go over the top in one final push.

'Yes, well,' I said.

'I hope you'll be very happy,' said Mark.

'It won't be long until I'm used to it,' I said. 'Skye's lovely. Blake's very good with him.' *It was just me whose heart was fracturing*. I took another deep breath. 'I hope all goes well for Jean. Give her my best wishes.'

'Thank you. I will.' We stood up, our food largely untouched. We left the canteen together, then he turned one way, back to Current Affairs, and I went the other to the empty, echoing spaces of Light Entertainment.

And I didn't feel brave, or noble, or self-sacrificing or any of those high-flown words.

I just felt like howling.

5

Blake was delighted when I told him I was pregnant. Mum was also pleased, reasoning that it would make the family properly complete. She reassured me that she'd be more than happy to look after both the children when it was time for me to go back to work.

I was . . . I was ambivalent. I found it desperately difficult, knowing I was carrying Mark's child and yet not being able to share it with him. Blake was caring and solicitous — rather too much so when he took charge of my diet, telling me what I should and shouldn't be eating to ensure the baby and I stayed healthy — but I knew I was playing a part. I hated being pregnant. I hated my body changing and none of my clothes fitting. I resented feeling tired all the time. I really disliked not being able to put a hundred percent effort into my work.

One of the problems was that none of my friends at work were anything like at the stage where they were producing children, so nobody understood my feelings. I began to realise why Jean had always been so anti the rest of us in the early years. I'd seen her just once since Mark broke the news. I was crossing the back of the foyer and she was sitting on one of the benches at the front with her two girls, obviously waiting for Mark. I put my head down and scuttled away, not wanting to analyse why I didn't want to talk to her, not wanting to swap cosy stages-of-pregnancy stories. Not wanting to see Mark's face as he greeted her and his daughters.

It wasn't just Jean, I was also avoiding Mark. I'd taken the decision that not seeing him at all would be safer than making artificial conversation and dissolving into an ocean of tears. It was easier than I'd expected because I realised he was avoiding me too. This actually made me feel worse. I missed his friendship so much. It was horrible, a great aching void in my life. I worked even harder to try not to notice it.

Blake didn't know me well enough to realise anything was wrong, but Mum did, even if she put it down to the pregnancy. 'What you need,' she said, looking at me thoughtfully, 'is a day at the health club with Kim.'

Kim was my sister-in-law. I protested feebly, but we were packed off and — wouldn't you know it — Mum was absolutely right. Kim — who you would have said was a shoe-in for all the mother of the year awards going — said yes, she loved the twins now, but before their birth she'd hated the idea of having a family. As we lay in the warm bubbling water and were then gently oiled and massaged, we let our hair down and oh, I did feel better.

'Thanks, Mum,' I said when I got back. 'You were right. I think I can cope now.'

One of the things Kim had told me to do was to join ante-natal classes as soon as I was offered them. Not just for the information, but to connect with other local women in the same situation as me.

'It gives you a safety group,' she explained. 'Everyone can moan amongst themselves and nobody judges you. I'm still in touch with my lot. We meet once a month or so to catch up and help each other and pat ourselves on the back about not killing anybody. That sort of thing.'

I took Kim's advice. It was good. None of the girls in my group hated being pregnant the way I did, none of them had a husband who was monitoring their health and trying to manage their pregnancy, but there were lots of smaller things we had in common and they really did make the last interminable stretch more bearable.

* * *

Ellie, bless her ten little pink toes, managed to hold on inside me until she was two weeks late. This made her two weeks *early* according to the fake dates I had given the hospital, so perfectly acceptable in everyone's eyes. Only the midwife awarded me a sharpish look, as if to say this was not a two-week-premature baby, but fortunately she didn't say anything. Blake had to rush off to a script meeting right after seeing Ellie into the world, due to nobody except me expecting her to arrive this soon, and that was good too. Why? Because my daughter's birth-wet hair dried to a blonde frizz, giving me one of those moments where your life flashes before your eyes.

'That won't last,' said the midwife, ruffling it.

It didn't. Within a couple of days it had fallen out, to be replaced by a safe, anonymous brown.

'You are a very clever girl,' I murmured to Ellie. 'We'll keep your daddy a secret just between us, shall we? Tuck those fair genes away.'

Ellie wrinkled her nose at me and I kissed it. As Kim had promised, the misery of being pregnant had faded already, leaving me with just a deep love for my daughter.

Skye was as fond of Ellie as I was, showing her off proudly as various relatives came to inspect her. Blake got a bit restive at this point. I'm not sure he'd realised quite how big my family was, or how many of them Skye was already familiar with. Mind you, I was restive too. Nice as it was being on maternity leave, I was ready to go back to work. I wasn't cut out to be a stay-at-home mother, and certainly Skye was happier and better adjusted when he was mixing with his cousins every day rather than just being at home with me. I reasoned Ellie would be the same.

Back into our routine again, Blake began to observe sourly that the children saw more of other people's parents than they did of their own. I shrugged it off, putting it down to him not being used to a large family. Another occasion on which I was entirely wrong.

Unlike some of the other husbands in

my support group, he enjoyed fatherhood. He was happy to look after the kids on the days when he worked from home. And if he did buy toys that were more educational than fun, well, it was his money.

I would have been quite happy to carry on the way we were indefinitely, but Blake suddenly announced that renting a flat was simply putting cash into other people's pockets and we should be buying our own place. To my dismay, he made a bid on a ghastly 1920s house in Finchley — cold, gloomy, oppressive and two long bus rides away from Mum.

'It's a terrific modernisation opportunity, Caro,' said Blake. 'We'd be mad not to go for it. We can decorate in the evenings when the children are asleep. Gallons of magnolia paint, storage units, and we'll knock the breakfast room into the scullery for a decent-sized kitchen. I can see it now, can't you?'

Trying not to make it sound like a criticism, I pointed out the difficulties with childcare.

He waved this away. 'We'll get an au pair. A pal of mine knows an agency. They cost hardly anything if you house them and teach them English. I'll be working from home a lot on this new series, so I can keep an eye on her.'

He'd already made his mind up. I didn't much like the idea, but having decided I owed it to him to be a good partner after using him to cover up Ellie's birth, I tried to be positive. I said it was important that the children still mixed with other kids regularly, so perhaps they could go to the tiny church nursery two or three times a week. How did that sound?

I was so naive. It took me ages to realise that the time I came back from work early with a splitting headache and found Blake with the au pair across his knee, it might not have just been because she'd run Skye's bath too hot that morning. I was horrified, of course, and furious with him. I said there were laws against chastisement and Astrid would have been within her rights to sue us. I said if he wasn't happy with her, I'd get up extra early and take the kids to Mum every day, no matter how difficult the journey. He replied that he didn't know what had come over him and it wouldn't happen again.

I had so many doubts during that time. Blake was an excellent father, but he really did like to be in control of everything. Astrid didn't seem to mind being bossed around. She grew glossy and insolent. I didn't like her, and suspected her of poking around in my wardrobe when everyone was out.

About a fortnight later she proved it.

I'd got as far the Tube station in the morning, when I realised I'd left the production schedule I'd been working on at home. Cursing, I hurried back, only to see Astrid walking the kids to the nursery wearing *my* green Biba platform shoes!

White hot fury engulfed me. 'I'll take the children from here,' I said, wrenching the pushchair out of her hands and leaving her standing on the pavement. 'You go and pack. You're fired. Take my shoes off before you leave.'

'Blake likes me to wear them,' she called after me.

I balanced Skye on the pushchair and *flew* it along the road to the church. Then I marched back. At home, Blake was looking annoyed. Presumably Astrid had interrupted his work, complaining about me.

'You can't just fire Astrid like that, Caro,' he said. 'What about the children? Who is going to look after them? I'm busy later.'

'I already have fired her,' I said crisply, dialling Mum's number. 'Domestic crisis, Mum. Can you pick up Skye and Ellie from the church hall and keep them for the rest of the day? I'll come to you after work if Dad doesn't mind giving us a lift home.' I looked, at Blake, still furious. 'There, that gives Astrid plenty of time to pack and get out of the house. I don't want to see her face ever again.'

'That's a little unreasonable, don't you think? Where's she going to find to sleep tonight?'

I shrugged. 'I don't care. She's got all day to look. I want my shoes back, any other clothes she's stolen and the front door key. If you are too busy to change the lock, I'll ask Dad to do it.' I pushed past Astrid to get to the study, picked up my production schedule and came back into the hall again, addressing her directly. 'Shoes. Off. Now. Those were given to me by my cousin. You chose the wrong pair to show off in.' I stormed along the hall to the front door and turned, looking at Blake this time. 'If she's still here when I get home with the kids this evening, I'm turning straight round with them and we'll go back to Mum's to sleep.'

I must have made my point, because Blake phoned me at work later. 'She's gone. The agency is sending someone else tomorrow.'

'Good,' I said. 'Have you changed the locks?' I was still angry.

His voice was very controlled, but I didn't care. 'Not yet. I'll get on to it now.' He paused. 'I didn't realise Jilly had given you those shoes.'

'Well, she did, which made it worse, but that's not the point. Astrid shouldn't have been wearing *anything* of mine. I have to go, Blake. I'll see you later.'

I found the shoes in the dustbin the next day, ripped to shreds. It didn't matter. I wouldn't ever have worn them again anyway.

★ ★ ★

Astrid was replaced by Danielle, a timid mouse of a girl who was wary of absolutely everything. She even asked permission when she wanted to make herself a coffee. She was fine with the kids as far as looking after them went, but she seemed to have no opinions of her own and her habit of dressing like a third world refugee and just sitting in a corner of the lounge every evening watching television in silence creeped me out.

'For goodness sake,' I said to Blake. 'She's single, twenty and in a foreign country. Why isn't she painting the town red in the evenings?' *Like I used to do not so very long ago.*

'You didn't like it when Astrid went out.'

'Astrid,' I said pointedly, 'was a completely different kettle of fish.'

'You're right. Danielle should be taking time to explore,' agreed Blake. 'She must have friends in London. I'll suggest it to her.'

Apparently, Danielle did have friends. Looking scared and furtively excited, she started going out a couple of times a week. There was even mention of a boyfriend. It was one of the periods when Blake was working late quite a lot, so it was wonderful having the house to myself again.

A couple of months later, however, I noticed Danielle's gaze was starting to follow Blake from under lowered lashes when he walked across a room. I also noticed the way she quivered when he patted her in absent approval after she'd learnt a new phrase or tidied the children's rooms especially well. There was, I thought cynically, no way Blake wouldn't have noticed these things as well. The question was, why hadn't he discouraged her crush on him? And the unpalatable answer? Presumably because he enjoyed it.

I suppose all marriages go through these problems. Was it my fault? It's true I was busy most of the time, but then, so was he. The decorating was virtually done now, but I still worked hard during the day because I didn't know any other way. When I was home, I spent time with the children. Blake and I didn't do anything together on our own.

None of which would have mattered if . . . I caught myself on the thought. Come on, Caroline, out with it . . .

None of which would have mattered if I'd been properly in love with him.

There. I'd admitted it to myself and it was bad. I was living with Blake as his wife under false pretences. I had accepted his ring solely for the respectability that having two legal parents

111

conferred on children. I'd liked him, of course, and it was clear he had fallen for me. I'd assumed that love would come in time. The fact that it hadn't so far, made no difference. I had a duty to make things work. I had an obligation. This wasn't something I could talk to Mum or Kim about. I'd have to sort it out myself. Be more loving towards Blake. Be more available. Talk to him more.

I did make an effort, and it did work to an extent, but Blake hated being chattered to in the mornings, he disliked being asked about his work, and on the evenings when he was home, he was also generally involved with the children.

Danielle grew even meeker in the face of my open lovingness. Her feebleness annoyed me intensely. I even had to stop myself being irritated by her long sleeves and high necks and opaque tights.

'Aren't you hot?' I snapped one morning. 'It is July, after all.'

She sidled away nervously.

Unfortunately, Danielle breaking up with her boyfriend coincided with Blake's annual climbing holiday, so I was stuck with her passive presence from the moment I got home in the evenings to the moment I went out in the mornings. She drooped so much I eventually gave her a week off out of sheer desperation and took the kids to stay with Mum. 'She's driving me demented,' I complained. 'Other families have cheerful Aussie au pairs who go to museums at weekends and take off every night to the pub with their friends. Why can't I have one of those? Danielle just drifts about the house giving great miserable sniffs and apologising for disturbing me. The only way I can escape from her is to catch the bus to see you.'

'Ah, I've been thinking about that,' said Mum. 'It's high time you learnt to drive now that you've got children to be responsible for. Your cousin Yvonne's new bloke is a driving instructor. Do you want a set of family-rate lessons as an early Christmas present?'

The freedom not to be dependent on public transport! 'Oh, Mum, yes please!'

When I returned home, relaxed after a loving, bickering week with the family, it didn't appear as if Danielle had done anything except lie on her bed eating chocolates. 'That girl,' I said to Blake when he arrived back looking tanned and fit following his three weeks in the mountains, 'has been about as much fun as a wet weekend.'

'Really? She seems all right now.'

'That's because you're back and you pay her wages.'

He preened. There was no other word for it. 'I'll have a word with her,' he said indulgently. 'Maybe she's had a row with her boyfriend.'

'She has,' I snapped. 'They've broken up. She hasn't been out once all the time you've been away.'

'Preposterous. I daresay it's all a misunderstanding. I'll talk to her.'

The next afternoon she humbly

asked permission to go out for the evening.

'Yes, of course,' said Blake without consulting me. 'I've got to go into town for a meeting. Would you like a lift?' He glanced at me as if to say *there, sorted, what was all the fuss about?*

I gave a tight-lipped smile back.

It seemed to do the trick. The day after her evening out she was almost embarrassingly eager to help, barely sitting down at all before springing up again. It was a nursery morning, so we were getting the kids ready to go out. Ellie was walking now, and had a habit of clutching at the nearest person for support. She grabbed the back of Danielle's thigh, making the girl yelp.

'Is something wrong?' I asked, glancing at her as I hoisted Ellie into the pushchair.

'I . . . I fell yesterday.' She mimed tripping. 'I hurt my . . . ' Her hand floated agitatedly in the region of her bottom.

'Oh, right. Well, be careful. Hope it

gets better soon.'

'Thank you.' She grasped the push-chair and set off along the road. Following behind them on my way to the Tube, I noticed she was indeed walking stiffly. I dismissed it from my mind and ran through the Highway Code in my head instead.

For once, Danielle didn't sidle into the lounge to watch television with us. Instead she asked if there was enough hot water for a bath. I replied impatiently that yes, of course there was, and she really didn't need to ask all the time.

Later I felt guilty, remembering her fall. Perhaps she'd wanted to soak her bruises. I got the arnica out of the medicine cabinet and tapped on her door. There was no answer, though I could hear the radio playing softly. I tapped again, a little louder. Still no answer. I opened the door a crack and looked in.

Danielle was asleep on the bed, lying on her front, stark naked. All across her bottom and the tops of her legs were masses of angry red stripes. Either she'd fallen down on a cattle grid yesterday — unlikely in the centre of London, I'd have thought — or her wretched boyfriend had very, very nasty tastes. I shut the door and leaned back against it, feeling sick.

'She needs to go home,' I said, going back downstairs again soberly.

Blake looked infuriated. 'Not again, Caro. What's the matter this time?'

My gut twisted. I knew these things happened of course, but I'd never met anyone who'd been schooled to enjoy pain before. I was eaten up with guilt for all the times I'd been irritated by Danielle instead of finding out what was wrong. 'I don't think she's got friends at all,' I said. 'I think she's in thrall to her horrible boyfriend and he beats her. No wonder the poor girl is terrified the whole while. She ought to be with her own family in her own country doing a proper job that uses up every scrap of time and gives her a sense of self-respect. Can you arrange it, Blake? There's no need to tell the agency why. And can we have a normal au pair next time, please? Is that too much to ask?'

6

It wasn't just at home things were changing. At work there were rumours of accountability, scaling back and outsourcing. The show I was working on was nearing the end of its run. Normally, I'd be assigned to something else in preparation at this stage, but on other projects people were clinging to their production jobs with the manic hands of those who could see the dole queue in their future. It wasn't looking good.

The BBC *was* commissioning externally though. Small, one-off programmes were creeping into the listings. It might not arrive just yet, but independent companies were likely to be the shape of things to come. I took a deep breath and when I was offered a redundancy package, I accepted.

Blake and I had discussed this, including the fact that it might take me a while to find a contract, but I hadn't told him *all* my plans. He was directing one of his own dramas at the time and having to stay in town for long hours, so I paid off au pair number three (a pert Austrian with the roundest, highest breasts I'd ever seen) and enrolled the kids in the local day nursery.

One of the church mums had told me about it. It had flexible hours to suit working parents and fed into the primary school Skye would be going to next September. It would, I said to Blake before he could get annoyed at the lack of consultation and argue with me, give Skye a head start because by then he would be used to full-time education in a play environment and he'd have already have made friends with the kids who would be going to the same school with him.

It would also give me time to pass my driving test and buy a small car while I sent out job applications. It was all very well Blake saying there was no need for me to learn since there were shops, buses and the station within walking distance and he would always be on hand to drive the kids further if necessary, but with my redundancy, the situation had now changed. Transport of my own was going to be essential for me as a freelancer. Not all television studios were handily situated next to Tube stations.

I didn't expect the new nursery to change my life, but it did. Ellie was a chatterbox of a child even then and had been talking about a new friend, Tori, incessantly. One day when I collected her and Skye, there she was in the home corner, dark hair messy as usual, hand in hand with a tiny blonde girl her own age. And crouching next to the pair of them, trying to persuade the blonde one to come home, was . . .

'Mark!' I said, a grin splitting my face. My whole body filled up with joy.

'Caro! I don't believe it!' He stood, his eyes lighting up with that wonderful warmth I remembered. 'What are you doing here?'

I couldn't prevent my utter pleasure at seeing him spilling over. 'Collecting the kids after a fruitless day's job-hunting. Skye, this is Mark, who I used to work with. I had no idea you and Jean lived around here.' In fact, I'd deliberately never looked for his address. I'd missed his friendship like a sold ache inside me, but there was no point messing up everyone's lives. Now though, two years on, both of us older, both of us with families, we could surely just be friends again, the way we'd been in the beginning?

'Skye, did you say? Jilly's boy?' Compassion touched Mark's voice.

'That's right. My boy now. Ellie, love, it's time to go home and have tea.'

Mark looked even more astounded. 'Caro, you're never telling me you are Ellie's mum? Jean will be delighted. She was saying we'd have to get this new Ellie over to play one weekend. Tori will keep talking about her. Do come back with us now and say hello. Have you got time?'

'Yes. That would be lovely if it's not too far,' I said. 'I haven't passed my driving test yet, so it's walk, bus or Tube. How have you been?' I was just so pleased to see him that I accepted without thinking. I could feel my heart unfurl within my chest, like a time-lapse bulb putting down new roots, growing leaves and stalks and buds and flowers. I honestly hadn't realised until I saw Mark again how miserable I'd been for the past two years without the daily contact. It was a revelation.

He felt the same, I could tell. 'Same as always,' he said with a shrug, but he was smiling as widely as me and I heard his voice singing under the words. 'Let's go, Tori. Ellie is coming with us.'

Skye walked next to me, with Mark on his other side. He peered between the two pushchairs where Ellie and Tori were still holding hands and said, 'Have I got two sisters now?'

Dear God, did my heart thump then! Out of the mouth of babes or what? 'No,' I said, too rapidly, too firmly and with a slightly high laugh. 'One is quite enough, don't you think?'

The shock jerked me back to my senses, though. God almighty, what on earth did I think I was doing? Casually strolling along like this with the unsuspecting father of my child. Perspiration prickled across my back. I wasn't in full command of my faculties at all. It was just as well Jean was going to be present or goodness only knew what I'd let spill in the giddiness of the moment.

Jean. She was the next hurdle. I had to admit I was less convinced of her likely delight at seeing me again than Mark was. We'd never particularly gelled in the old days, even though, since my own pregnancy experience, I now understood why.

However, it seemed I'd wronged her. Jean *was* pleased. Unlike me, she was in her element as a wife and mother, never happier than when dispensing advice on all child-related matters, and busily useful on the PTA and nursery committees. She was the epitome of a neat blonde earth-mother, queen of the PTA cake stall and baby sitting rota.

'I don't know how you do it,' I said over tea and home-made flapjacks. 'I've only been unemployed a fortnight and I'm already at screaming point. Even the wasteland of the Light Entertainment department was better than chasing job applications. Did you hear the BBC had dispensed with my services, Mark?'

Mark grinned from his position on the sofa where his two older girls were cuddled one either side of him reading him their school storybooks, a page at a time, alternately. 'More fool them,' he said. 'I wonder . . . I might be able to help. The tiny indie I've been moonlighting for have been let down and need a production coordinator as soon as possible. They can't pay much, mind.'

'You life-saver. I can start tomorrow. Have you got a phone number for them?'

* * *

125

That was the start of my career with the independents. It was also the start of a lifelong friendship between Ellie and Tori. Rarely was one of them seen without the other throughout their childhood and adolescence.

Jean was inclined to fuss about this as they grew up. 'It's not healthy, being so fixated on each other,' she said. 'Suppose they turn out to be gay?'

'If they are, I couldn't wish for nicer in-laws,' I replied. This wasn't quite what Jean wanted to hear, but she was used to me by now and just glared and muttered that I wasn't taking it seriously.

The months went by and I kept pushing to the back of my mind the circumstances of Ellie's conception. I knew I should tell Mark, and I was going to, of course I was, but the thought of the upset it would cause between our families filled me with such absolute horror that I quailed before it. Being completely honest with myself, I also really dreaded the prospect of losing Mark's friendship just when I had it back again. This was selfish, and it did bother me, but having him in my life was keeping me sane and I was clear-sighted enough to know he would always choose Jean and the girls over me, no matter what his personal feelings were. He'd made a promise, he had commitments, just as I had. We were still honourable people.

Just after Skye started school, there was even more reason not to rock the boat. Mark was also made redundant. He'd secured one research contract to tide himself over. Now he was panicking about where the next one was coming from.

'Well . . . ' I said, eyeing him warily.

'Well what? I'm at my wit's end, Caro. It's not like it was with you and Blake. We don't have any other money coming it at all apart from what I earn.'

'Well . . . ' I repeated, and broached my big idea. Which was, quite simply, to start our own company. Him and me, together. It would make us more visible in the industry marketplace. It would keep more of the contract money in our own hands.

The thing was, I'd discovered I really liked not having the restraints of the BBC around me and that I was even better at my job than I'd thought. I suspected Mark would be the same. Production assistance and research assistance were often needed together, and when they weren't, we could work on separate projects.

The independent company I'd been working for most recently had had an idea for a quiz show that could use us both, but they didn't want to bear the whole cost if it didn't take. If we bought into it, it would be a good place to begin.

Surprisingly, Blake was all in favour of us going solo. To be honest, I think he was keen on anything that kept me busy. I got in the way at home. 'You need a strong name,' he said. 'Something catchy. Let me think . . . *LineMark*? It's a concatenation of Caroline and Mark. It sounds trustworthy. It'll look good on the credits.'

'You're the man with the words,' said Mark easily.

'You'll need an office.' Jean was very firm on this point. She had her own routines, her own coteries, and it put her out terribly with Mark being either under her feet or working with all his papers spread out on the dining room table. 'It's more professional,' she added.

I agreed with her. I didn't want to work from home any more than Blake wanted to have me there when he was pacing the house writing. I needed people around me. I needed the radio on or a TV monitor playing. I needed bustle, telephones, fax machines and clattering typewriters. We wouldn't get that for a while, but we could make a start. Camden Town had cheap, disused warehouses, an NW1 postcode, easy access from Finchley on the Northern line, and equally simple travel from there into town. Mark and I put our bank loans together, rented a ground floor suite, installed a phone and hired a secretary. Then we bought business cards, designed ourselves some headed stationery, and we were off.

Our first year was very scary indeed, but the quiz show was a success, a second series was commissioned, other work came in and by the time Ellie and Tori had started primary school, we were cautiously expanding. We did ask Jean whether she wanted to come and do part-time secretarial stuff in the front office, but she looked askance at us and said this was the first free time she'd had in God knows how many years and she was too busy going to the gym and joining dance classes and generally regaining her fitness to go to work.

When she later told Mark she'd got a job on the reception at the local leisure centre — just as our workload exploded and we could have really done with some extra help — he heroically sealed his lips and said nothing.

★ ★ ★

Lost in memories, I hadn't realised how long I'd been sitting in the darkening lounge. I rose stiffly from my armchair, put back Jilly's letters, tucked away the set of David Bowie postcards I'd bought from the V&A as a reminder and got ready for bed. Blake hadn't returned. He'd be staying at his club overnight. He'd started doing it years ago, saying it would save disturbing me and the children when he came in after a late recording session. I'd thought at the time it was probably a peace-making gesture following my getting so fed up with having au pairs in the house and putting my foot down about not having any more. It was all very well him being patriarchal and lord of all he surveyed, but it wasn't good for the kids being cooped up here all the time and I'd hated the feeling of being a cipher in my own home. I'd not made a fuss on the first occasion when Blake stayed in town, and the arrangement had continued. It was convenient on many levels. On any awards evening, for example, when he failed once again to run out as the winner after being shortlisted, it was especially convenient.

Blake was not a good loser, no matter how many times he put on an above-it-all face for the world at large and said what an honour it was that his work was considered one of the top three (or five or seven) dramas of the year.

I remember one lunchtime at the BBC, soon after we'd got married. Blake had been shortlisted for something reasonably prestigious and one of the top brass had paused by the table where we were eating. He'd congratulated Blake on flying the flag for the BBC drama and had added that Blake was almost becoming a resident in these media awards and it was nice to have a reliable BBC presence.

I'd swelled with reflected praise, which just shows how little I'd known. Blake had thanked the man urbanely, but underneath he'd been furious. 'I don't write them so the bloody BBC can have a reliable presence,' he'd ground out, mashing his cottage pie to oblivion with his fork. 'I write them because the stories are *there*.'

'Yes, of course, but the shortlist publicity can't harm when it comes to commissioning the next one, can it?' I said. 'One has to live, after all.'

He'd looked at me as if I was a stranger (which, of course, I was). 'My work is commissioned because it's good,' he said coldly.

I'd back-pedalled, it being a bit soon in our relationship to have an argument on the practicalities of life in the middle of the BBC canteen. 'You know that and I know that,' I said, 'but accountants only see the figures, not the art.'

'Money isn't everything, Caro.'

I prudently took a large bite of my quiche, on the grounds that I'd been brought up not to talk with my mouth full.

I never went to awards evenings with him. The first time the question had arisen, he was up for a short-drama award for a dark, twisted story of obsession. It had got good reviews, but I'd found it unwatchable, so I was thankful for the excuse of being pregnant and having Skye to look after not to go.

I commiserated with Blake the next morning. He shrugged, telling me he could live with it. Apparently, he'd left early, livid with the judges' obtuseness, but on letting himself into the flat, he'd seen me and Skye curled up together fast asleep and had known he was the real winner. It was one of the nicest things he's ever said to me.

In fact I wasn't keen on any of Blake's dramas. They were the sort of clever, psychological, uncomfortable pieces that were much in vogue at the time, but they made my skin crawl. I let it be known that I admired him enormously for writing them, but that I didn't think I was brainy enough to appreciate them properly. He smiled and said I had other attributes that made me desirable and not to concern myself about it. After all, he added kindly, he rarely watched the sort of shows I worked on, but that didn't mean he couldn't appreciate the skill that went into running them.

★ ★ ★

My brow creased now as I slowly got ready for bed. I'd been thinking Blake and I had grown apart, but when I looked back properly, we'd never really been soul-mates in the first place. All we'd ever had in common had been the children. With them grown up and having moved away to homes of their own, we didn't even have that any more.

We still shared the house, of course, and decades of memories. We also had a social life and an assumption of couple-ness. Without my work, though, my actual life here was empty. Were we the only ones like this? How many other people stayed together out of habit?

Jean had, it seemed. I'd been flabbergasted when she told me she was going out to Portugal with Fernando. I didn't see how anyone could possibly get bored with Mark — I hadn't, in all the years we'd been working together — but she'd said there was no excitement with him, no feeling of being cherished and she'd been having an affair for ages.

'We had the children too young,' she explained airily. 'You know I didn't have any 'me space' until Tori went to school.' She paused. 'Mind you, at the time she was my master stroke.'

'Sorry?' I replied.

She'd given me a look, half guilty, half triumphant. 'Seven-year itch.'

I shook my head. 'You've lost me.' They'd been married for considerably longer than seven years.

'I thought Mark was getting the seven-year itch,' she explained. 'You can always tell, can't you? I panicked. Well, I wasn't trained for anything, was I? I'd had Lydia straight from school. All I knew about was running a house and bringing up children. So I got pregnant again. That stopped him straying.'

I must have gaped at her. 'Oh, come on, Caro,' she said impatiently. 'Don't tell me you've never done anything less than perfect to keep your marriage going.'

'I . . . no,' I said.

Jean looked at me in disbelief and changed the subject to how she knew Fernando wasn't perfect, but at least he wasn't bloody polite to her all the time.

I let it wash over me, stunned. Mostly I was thinking *what a waste, what a waste, what a waste of all our years.* But I still didn't do anything about it because I'd made that promise to Blake.

Now, I wondered. The reason I'd never had to resort to desperate measures like Jean was because Blake had never shown the slightest inclination to leave me. Why not? Why had he been attracted to me in the first place? We were so very unalike. Unless that's what he wanted, of course — a busy, bustling livewire as a contrast to his cerebral, orderly life. He was always the one in charge though. He allowed me my flamboyant cushions, but kept the walls magnolia. He put up with a modicum of clutter, but confined it to a corner of each room. He came to my family gatherings (occasionally with a long-suffering air), but he didn't instigate them. And yet . . . and yet we rubbed along. We might not have taken an interest in each other's jobs, but we respected them. Blake had certainly always had my welfare at heart — witness that time he vetoed the suggestion that I should work on a documentary being made about Alessandro's commune out in Italy.

'No, Caro,' he'd said. 'It will bring it all back. You'll get terribly upset, thinking about Jilly.'

I'd fingered the letter. 'Alessandro says we can all go out, you and the children as well, have a bit of a holiday. He'd like to see Skye.'

Blake had looked appalled. 'It would upset Skye even more than it would you! No, Caro, thank him for the thought and walk away. Send him another photograph.'

So that's what I'd done, but I still think Blake was wrong. Skye hadn't even been a year and a half when he'd left Italy, and he'd always known about Jilly and that I'd adopted him. He might have been distressed by me getting teary when we were out there, but that was all. As for me, sufficient time had passed by then that I'd have been able to see the Castello though Jilly's eyes.

It wasn't worth a row though. I declined the job and we went to Cornwall as usual for our family holiday. And even when Blake went off on his climbing weeks without us, I'd respected his concerns and not taken the children to the Castello by myself.

Once upon a time, I'd thought there would be so much more to life than a succession of small interactions, that there would be more to look back on than a long list of compromises.

I sighed. And that, finally, was why

I'd been reluctant to visit those early memories today. I'd never dreamt that keeping promises would be so draining. But there you are. I could have changed my circumstances, but I didn't. I'd made my choice. I'd failed the girl I was.

My gaze fell on the photographs on my dressing table.

Except for the children.

I smiled, my heart lightening. It was true. The children were a triumph.

7

I still remember the day Skye told me he was gay. It was such a relief to have it out in the open. I'd guessed which way things were going for some time, of course, and had tried to let him know I was fine with it. I couldn't say it in as many words — not until he'd said it first — but I consciously projected a tolerant attitude whenever same-sex relationships were shown on television, mentioned in the newspapers or came up in general conversation. It turned out Skye wasn't at all worried about my reaction, but he was terrified of telling Blake.

'Dad gets so weird about things when they don't happen like he expects them to,' he said, having finally come into the office after Sixth Form College one day to blurt it out.

'This is true,' I replied, remembering several explosive episodes, 'but all he's ever wanted is for you to be happy.'

Skye slanted a look at me remarkably reminiscent of Jilly. 'Happy and successful,' he corrected, 'and better than anyone else.'

'There is that,' I allowed.

Skye moved restlessly about the room. 'And he always thinks he knows best exactly how Ellie and I should be happy and successful and better than anyone else. Do you know he's made her a revision timetable *already* for her GCSEs? He's going to go mental when he finds out she's lost it.'

'I have known your sister for fifteen years. I took a copy. Stop changing the subject. Skye, darling, I can't do this for you. You'll have to tell Dad yourself, man to man, in your own words. No trimmings, no excuses, just how it is. He'll appreciate that.' I paused. 'You can give him your mock A-level results at the same time.'

Skye had laughed, throwing his head back just like Jilly always used to do. 'I do love you, Mum. Are you nearly finished? Can I have a lift home?'

'You mean, can you practice driving my car home? Go and put the L-plates on, then. I'll be with you in ten minutes.'

'Thanks.' Still he'd fidgeted. 'Is Mark in? I might try out my words on him first.'

He wandered down the passage and I heard Mark's door open. Like a conscientious mother, I didn't listen, but I couldn't fail to hear Mark's reply.

'At bloody last. Maybe you'll be happier with yourself now. Well done on your mocks, by the way. Caro told me. Listen, Skye, these Schools of Architecture you're looking at — check out the social side as well as the course content, okay? Some places aren't as sympathetic as others.'

'I will. I'm including some looking-around time on the open days. Thanks, Mark.'

Blake took longer to come to terms with the news, but I'd known he'd accept it. In Blake's eyes, despite those explosive episodes, Skye had rarely put a foot wrong his whole life. He probably thought he'd chosen his sexual orientation deliberately to save Blake from ever having to lose Skye to a daughter-in-law.

That being the case, I was honestly shocked a few months later to discover that Blake's next TV drama featured a troubled gay relationship as the central theme.

Skye shrugged, resigned, when I indignantly pointed it out to him. 'I expected that. He always does it, hadn't you noticed? That Christmas when Laura and Darren had that huge fight at Granny's and Darren was effing and blinding about the cost of Laura's dress and Laura was screaming at the top of her voice detailing every single thing he'd done wrong during their entire marriage — all that went into *Thread of Jade*.'

'No! Honestly?'

'Yes. Didn't you watch it?'

I made a face. 'I never do. Give me a nice game show any day.'

* * *

Skye brought Rob home the first Christmas after he started at university. They finished each other's sentences like a tag team as they told me how they'd come together, so much love between them it took me by the throat with happiness and I ached that Jilly would never see it. It seemed Rob had been serving in the student bar when Skye had walked in at the beginning of term and their eyes had met across the pandemonium. Two hours later, Rob had escaped from behind the counter on the pretext of clearing tables, come straight across to where Skye was sitting and said something along the lines of 'Why, aye, bonny lad, my name's Rob. What's yours?'

He'd lost the bar job the same night, due to talking solidly to Skye for the rest of the evening, but then got it back again the next day by dint of turning up for work as if nothing had happened.

'But it did, Mum,' said Skye.

'I can see that,' I replied, kissing them both, joy melting me.

Rob stayed with us every holiday after that. His own people had thrown him out. The family pub that had been home all his life didn't want 'his sort' on the premises, no matter how thick the blood ties or how hard a grafter he was.

Rob's life-plan was simple. He wanted to open his own bar and brasserie. He was doing a degree in business management because he already knew how to cook but he didn't know how to run a catering establishment profitably. He was making sure of the student grant for the difficult half of the plan before he tackled the easy bit. Meanwhile, he was keeping his hand in behind the student bar in order to live.

'You working during your spare time makes me feel guilty and privileged,' said Skye, but Rob nudged his shoulder good-naturedly.

'You haven't got time to get a job, bonny lad,' he said. 'Not with the amount of prep you have to do. You've got another six or seven years' bloody hard work in front of you. Then you'll be designing beautiful spaces, earning a fortune and can bankroll my bar.'

Skye grinned. 'Fair enough.'

After finishing his own degree, Rob took a job in a hotel kitchen near the university until Skye graduated, then Skye found a placement in a London practice and studied for his final exams while Rob honed his craft in a dream post in a Michelin star restaurant. Blake was in his element, dropping 'my son the architect' into casual conversation and referring to 'my son's partner, the graduate chef'.

It was a severe shock to him when Skye told us he was joining an architect's practice in Cambridge where Rob was opening up his new bistro.

'It'll give us space to breathe,' Skye whispered in my ear. 'Even Dad can't do London to Cambridge in less than ninety minutes.'

★ ★ ★

147

If Blake had taken a while to accept Rob as Skye's partner, it was nothing to how he felt about Ellie's eventual choice.

Ellie was the original rebel. She and Tori enjoyed music, dancing, concerts of all kinds and clubbing. Each of them went through a succession of unsuitable boyfriends with breathtaking speed.

For myself — noticing how Ellie dropped each boy as soon as Blake cultivated an interest in him — I was fairly convinced it was just high spirits, the knowledge that they were young and beautiful, and a healthy excess of energy. This was borne out one night when Blake emerged from his study just as Ellie got home, demanding to know what she was doing back this late and he'd seen her kissing that biker in the road outside and did the said biker know she was underage?

Ellie, never one to hold back if an argument was in the offing, retorted that coming back late was better than not coming back at all, the kiss was to say thanks for the lift, and that she'd only been dancing, for goodness sake, what on earth did he think she'd been doing? She'd been brought up better than that, hadn't she? It was his fault if she hadn't.

Blake went white. '*What* did you say?' he grated.

In a lightning change of mood, she balanced on tiptoe and kissed his cheek. 'It was only dancing, Dad. Night night.'

She ran upstairs, her energy undiminished. Blake got his breathing under control and fired a furious glance at me. 'Those girls are going to be impossible over the summer holidays. It's no good you saying your mother will have them — she's never stopped thinking kids should play outside all year long. Can Jean get them jobs at the leisure centre?'

'There's no need to worry,' I said. 'We've already agreed that I'm hiring them as runners from the day after school breaks up. They'll be so busy they won't even have time to spend the money they'll be earning.'

Blake harrumphed and disappeared back into his study. I sighed at the closed door. Now what was wrong? The fact that Ellie was having fun? The fact that I'd sorted her out for the summer without consulting him? The fact that she'd argued with him? It could be anything.

Ellie had a beautiful voice and she'd always enjoyed the TV buzz whenever she'd worked for me, so when she announced she was going to specialise in performing arts for her A-levels, I wasn't surprised. Then her GCSE results came in surprisingly high, so she switched to business studies, doing music and amateur dramatics on the side. Remembering my own experience, I enrolled her on a touch-typing course which she flew through. After she'd got thoroughly bored in a couple of dead-end jobs, a several-times-removed cousin on my father's side got her a position as an academic secretary at Imperial College and she moved out to share a tiny flat with Tori who was doing nursing and midwifery at University College Hospital.

Far from being pleased about these promising signs of settling down, Blake was disgruntled that once again, my family had turned up trumps in finding her employment when none of his own suggestions had borne fruit.

'Honestly, Blake,' I said, 'there are so many of us, it would be surprising if *no one* could help on any given occasion. The entire world runs on nepotism. Why shouldn't Duncan put forward a family connection for an interview if a suitable job comes up in his department? Everyone else does. She got the job on her own merits after that.'

I carefully didn't mention that Duncan was quite good-looking in a dark, sultry, reformed-pirate fashion. It would be nice if something came of it, but most unfortunately he washed regularly, had more than a nodding relationship with the barber, and held down a good job. These circumstances alone would keep him off Ellie's boyfriend list if the last few years were anything to go by.

Blake may have come to the same conclusion. At any rate he was soothed, right up until the moment we were watching the Last Night of the Proms on television and saw Ellie and Duncan, in the middle of the promenaders, kissing foursquare in the centre of the screen. Not just any old kiss either. This one clearly meant it.

The phone rang almost instantly. Lifting the receiver, I could hear the same programme in the background. 'I didn't know Ellie was seeing Duncan!' yelled Skye in my ear.

I eyed the screen where both Ellie and Duncan were looking rather dazed. 'I don't think they did either,' I replied.

⋆ ⋆ ⋆

Now I chuckled as I got into bed and turned off the light. It was funny, looking back on it, but it hadn't been at the time. Mark had rung me straight after Skye put the phone down, and I'd no sooner told him I'd let him know what was going on once I'd talked to Ellie herself, than Mum was on the phone with the same question, closely followed by Aunty Pam. Blake's temper had got shorter with each call. I'd had to miss the rest of the programme and take the phone into the kitchen in the end.

Duncan and Ellie still go to the Last Night of the Proms every year, taking the kids with them. I remember vividly when Oliver was born. Ellie had been fretting that she'd miss their Albert Hall anniversary as that was when she was about due. Tori exercised her midwifery divination skills and declared the baby would be born with a couple of weeks to spare, and so it had proved. Mind you, the moment of wide-eyed shock when they all realised Oliver had a mop of tow-coloured hair was wonderful to behold.

'Ellie!' said her friend with a shriek.

'Come on, Tori,' I said. 'You must have seen that before. It often happens. Ellie was born with fair hair herself. It darkened later, but even if it hadn't, a family as large as ours has got every gene going somewhere. It's pure lottery which ones make their way into the egg.'

'That,' said Tori, 'is a brilliant explanation. I'll keep it for my other mothers. Also for the fathers.'

I went to make phone calls to the family, leaving Tori to tidy up and Duncan, Ellie and Oliver to bond. Maybe it was the adrenalin spike of seeing my daughter safely through childbirth, but I felt surprisingly deflated now it was over. She'd grown up at last. I remembered the heart-stopping moment when I first set eyes on her own head of fair hair. Where had the years gone?

I said as much to Mark when I rang him with the news. 'It's a boy. Tori says mother and baby are both doing well. Tori was very good, by the way. Ellie and Duncan are over the moon.'

'That's great,' said Mark. 'And how are you?'

'I feel awfully old. It doesn't seem more than a moment since Ellie was born herself.'

'I know, but we're not old really, Caro. We're not even approaching our prime. Give Ellie my love. Is Blake pleased he's got a grandson?'

My heart skipped a beat as I realised I'd automatically rung Mark first. 'I haven't told him yet,' I said. 'I'll send him a text. He hates being disturbed when he's writing and I wanted a proper conversation.' *Talking too much, Caroline. Stop now while you're still above water.*

There was a small pause during which Mark tactfully didn't ask what man minded being disturbed when his daughter had just been safely delivered of a baby. 'A proper conversation before you call your mum and can't get a word in edgeways, you mean? Okay, I'll see you later if you manage to get into the office.'

* * *

I sighed. That was also all in the past now. As Mark had said this morning, even the grandchildren were growing up fast, with lives busier than one of my production schedules. Oliver was nearly twelve and Ellie and Duncan had just bought their own 'renovation opportunity', a run-down family house with a garden backing onto the railway line. They were having the housewarming this weekend, complicated by there being a charity concert in the community centre the same evening that Sasha, their youngest, was singing in.

This clashing of events was the stuff of life to Ellie. 'The concert will clear the place nicely,' she'd said, calling into the office after sourcing off-beat decorations for the party from Camden Market. 'Someone can stay behind to let Skye and Rob in. It's a shame they can't get away before Rob's finished prepping for the evening.'

I raised my eyebrows. 'And I suppose

this someone might clear up all your guests' used glasses and put the dish-washer on and lob the joint in the oven for later?'

She grinned at me. 'Love you, Mum.'

★   ★   ★

Blake was furious about Ellie's new house, largely because she and Duncan hadn't consulted him, even more so since he'd discovered they *had* asked Duncan's father what he thought about the purchase. That they'd also consulted Skye regarding the soundness of the structure didn't count.

'It'll be much too noisy with the trains running late into the night and it's also completely unsafe with just that scrubby bank down to the track,' he said again at breakfast on Saturday when I raised the question of what time we should leave. 'Skye's apartment in Cambridge is far better value for money. It'll be worth a fortune when all the new building in the area is finished.'

'So will Ellie's house be, once they've done it up,' I replied. 'They probably won't even hear the noise from the trains after the first couple of weeks. That wire fence along the back means there's no danger of the kids tumbling onto the track by accident. Children need a garden to run about in, Blake. Look at the fun Oliver and Sasha always have here. It's not something Skye and Rob are ever going to have to worry about.'

He opened the paper, shutting me out. He was cross anyway because of getting a rejection for a proposed mini-series yesterday. As I ran the water for the washing up, I thought of Ellie and Duncan, laughing together, occasionally yelling, but above all *talking* to each other all the time. We never did. Not properly. It was a marriage of habit and convenience.

This isn't living, I thought despairingly. What had happened to the colourful future I'd once assumed lay in store for me? Was that why Jean had left? Because she wasn't where she'd wanted to be?

'I went to the V&A the other day,' I

said, trying to talk myself away from the grey stretch of forever that had opened up with horrid presentiment in front of my eyes. 'They've got a David Bowie exhibition going right back to the early years.'

Silence. Blake continued to drink his coffee and read the paper as if answering me was unimportant. Normally this didn't bother me, but today I came over all Ellie-like. I wanted to rattle him, make him talk to me. I wanted to shake the all-too-familiar feeling that I might as well not be here. 'You were in one of the photos, watching the band and arguing with Jilly. I didn't think you knew her that well.'

He turned a page in crisp irritation, folded it neatly back on itself. 'I was going to marry her,' he said.

The plate I was washing dropped out of my hand into the water. My hand followed it. As I turned to look at Blake, astounded, I felt the water lapping my wrist, felt my hand heating with the temperature while the other one pressed fingertips into the draining board to keep me anchored to reality.

'Marry Jilly?' I said. 'You were going to marry Jilly? You've never told me that before.'

He continued to read. 'There was no need to tell you. It didn't happen. She went travelling.' His voice was flat and dead. Indifferent.

'Oh come on, Blake, you can hardly blame her for that. She was twenty two and wanted to see the world.'

'It was most inconsiderate of her.'

Inconsiderate. What a very Blake word. 'Is that why you chose me, then?' I asked flippantly. 'Because I'm more reliable?'

I shouldn't have goaded him. I'd known he was cross, and he's always hated being interrupted whilst reading the paper. He turned another page with an annoyed rattle of paper.

'No, I married you because you had adopted Skye.'

8

I married you because you had adopted Skye.

It was a misstep so profound and astonishing that I gasped aloud. For a full ten seconds the world stopped in its tracks. Blake's words were as much of a shock as all those years ago when we heard the news about those three astronauts stranded in Apollo 13. I felt again the sheer incredulity at the realisation that something I had always taken for absolute truth (*Blake loves you, the space programme is safe*) turned out to be entirely opposite. 'You married me to be close to *Skye*?' I repeated with disbelief. 'Blake, is this a joke?'

'I married you in order to be Skye's father,' Blake corrected. He looked at me dispassionately. It was his writer's face, distant and apart, as if he was recording my reaction for potential use later. 'It's not a joke, Caro. Why would it be? The ridiculous stipulation Jilly wrote into her will meant I couldn't adopt him in my own right, which I assure you would have been my first move otherwise. That was really very thoughtless of her. I'm still angry about it. The way things stood, marrying you was a simpler option than getting blood tests done and contesting the adoption in court. You weren't Jilly, of course, but I couldn't help that. She was gone. I wasn't going to lose my son as well.'

'Your son?'

'Certainly. I knew Skye was my son as soon as you told me he was Jilly's child. I'd taken steps, you see. His February birthday confirmed it. Jilly may have been secretive about her plans, but she wasn't seeing anyone else. I'd have noticed.'

'Oh,' I said faintly. I hadn't even known she was seeing Blake. How could she never have mentioned it? This was wrong, it had to be. Reality was streaming away from me, like sand slipping through my frantically clutching fingers.

'I've thought about it a great deal since,' Blake went on. 'The pregnancy must have been why she continued with the travelling. Most people would have come home in a situation like that, but I've observed how women's hormones frequently have a destabilising effect. Making you the boy's guardian, for example. That was decidedly eccentric, but I could turn it to my advantage. You seemed a biddable girl. You were young enough to be malleable. I didn't anticipate you being any trouble, certainly less trouble than any of my other girlfriends.' He paused, his eyes reflective. 'I hadn't bargained on your family, but again, I've had my money's worth out of them over the years by way of incidents and characters to use in my work. No, it was simple. I just had to tell you I loved you, have sex frequently enough to keep you docile, provide not quite enough money to manage the house and make sure you stayed busy earning the rest yourself.' He looked at me calmly. 'You've surprised me on several occasions, Caro. I was really very annoyed when you kept interfering over the au pairs, for example. But in general it hasn't been too difficult or displeasing. I've been quite comfortable.'

I stared at him, feeling more nauseous than I would have believed possible. 'I don't know what to say, Blake,' I stammered. 'Everything I thought . . . everything I knew . . . For thirty-seven years I've thought you loved me, at least to begin with. I've based our life on that. I'm not sure I can live with you any more.'

As the words stumbled out, release flooded me. The shackles of loyalty, so long worn I hardly noticed how they were weighing me down, crumbled to dust.

Blake sat back, considering my statement. 'Where will you go?'

He wasn't even going to argue with

me. Thirty-seven years and he wasn't even going to argue. I really was a ghost presence here, of no use or interest except as a long-ago means to an end. 'I don't know,' I said, clamping down on rising hysteria. 'I'll move into the flat above the office for now. I'm sorry, Blake. I know it must seem illogical when we've been sharing the house and the children for so long. It's just that our whole life together has been based on a lie. That's a really big thing to absorb. I need time to come to terms with it.'

He frowned. 'Skye is arriving this evening. How are you going to explain not being here?' Again, he wasn't arguing, just asking for information, synchronising our stories for the family.

'He and Rob are staying at Ellie's tonight,' I said. 'They can't get down for very long, so he promised Oliver and Sasha he'd maximise the time spent with them in the morning. We don't need to say anything today about me moving out, Blake. It would spoil the housewarming.'

'Well, you'll have to live here while I'm away climbing. I'm not having the house empty. It's an open invitation to burglars.'

Again, I clamped down on a scream. 'I can do that. I can pack the rest of my stuff at the same time.'

Unbelievably, he returned to the newspaper, as if I was a piece of business that he'd needed to clear out of the way while he thought of it. 'You realise people will talk.'

I shook my head. 'Not these days. Couples often grow apart, especially once the family has left home. There's no shame in it, Blake. Hardly any of our friends are still with their original partners. It won't even be a nine days' wonder.'

★   ★   ★

Mark stared at me, appalled. 'Blake only married you to be Skye's father?'

I shakily poured myself another mug

166

of tea. We were in the office. I'd thrown clothes, photos, letters and shoes into the car more or less at random and driven straight to Camden Town. I hadn't even realised I'd rung Mark until I heard his voice answering the phone. He'd come in straight away.

A memory surfaced. Blake's voice, gently bracing. *It's tragic, Caro, but you have to concentrate on Skye now. He's the important one.* Had he even then been planning, calculating, preparing to ensnare me? Yes, yes of course he had.

'All these years he's kept it hidden,' I said. 'He's kept up the pretence. He courted me, charmed my family to get them on side, fooled me into caring and married me — all in order to be Skye's father in the eyes of the law. He lied, all that time. He did it to bring Skye up, to have constant access to him, to . . . to own him. He's convinced himself he's Skye's natural father. He must have decided to marry me the moment he found me crying in the BBC canteen and I told him Skye was Jilly's little boy.' I dashed a hand across my eyes. 'I've been so stupid, Mark. To hear him talk this morning, you'd think he never loved me at all. Everything has always been for Skye. Do you remember when he came down so hard against us doing the documentary on Alessandro's commune that time? I bet even that wasn't to save me from bad memories, it was to protect Skye. Maybe he was jealous at the thought that Alessandro might want to do more godfathering. They take those duties a lot more seriously in Italy.'

Mark wrapped my hand in both his in silent sympathy.

I laughed miserably. 'I'll be okay. A lot of this is the blow to my self-esteem. I feel so *used*. I've stayed with him out of duty all these bloody years . . . and for what? Probably the real reason he bought the blasted house in Finchley was simply to get the kids away from Mum and the family — and properly under his control.'

'Speaking selfishly, I'm glad he did,' said Mark. 'We might never have reconnected otherwise. Do the dates work? Could he actually be Sky's father?'

I shook my head. 'No. I know Jilly wasn't pregnant before she left, because she took all the tampons with her. I remember going to the cupboard where they were kept and finding nothing. That's when it sunk in that she'd really gone and the flat was mine.'

'She might have been pregnant without realising.'

'I honestly don't think so. She knew who Skye's father was, and he didn't sound like Blake from the letters I found later. Also, she never even mentioned him to me in any romantic context. Did she to you?'

Mark shook his head.

'I suppose the timing is just possible,' I went on, 'only just, but it's really unlikely in any case. Blake's been firing blanks ever since I've known him.'

The words fell out as I spoke my

thoughts aloud, unguarded for the first time since I'd walked down the aisle to the altar. A deadly silence rose from the place where they lay stranded. Too late, I heard what I'd said. I covered my face with my hands. *Oh, well done, Caroline. Today of all days.*

'Caro?' said Mark quietly.

I took a shallow breath and met his eyes. 'I didn't mean to say that. I certainly never meant to say it that badly. Oh God, I'm sorry, Mark. There's no easy way to tell you this. Ellie isn't Blake's daughter.' I took another breath. 'She's yours.'

There was more shock on his face then than I have ever seen on anyone. 'I'm sorry,' I repeated wretchedly. 'I know I should have said something years ago. The thing is, I didn't even think about possible consequences that night. Jilly was dead and you were there. Both of us needed comfort. I wasn't on the Pill.'

'Caro . . . '

'Jilly wasn't on the Pill either, come

to that. I found a box of condoms in the bedside table after I moved in, but they'd all perished. Little holes in the ends. I threw them away.'

He wasn't deflected. 'Caro, why the hell didn't you let me know?'

My voice rose. 'I was going to. Of course I was going to. But when I came back from Italy, you were on your way to Margate with Jean and the girls. Where you caught mumps, if you remember, and were then off work for weeks. Meanwhile I'd missed a period, been fired, got reinstated, changed departments, Blake was making this enormous, flattering play for me, there was pressure from the family and Skye wouldn't let me out of his sight. My life was upside down, Mark. I was panicking so hard and I didn't know what to do. You were ill and I couldn't phone you or write to you and even if I had, it wouldn't have been fair on Jean . . . ' I stopped. 'Not getting in touch with you then was the most difficult thing I had ever done in my life. I was twenty years old, overwhelmed, inexperienced and very, very scared. You were out of reach and besides, it would have been wrong. Blake said he wanted to take care of me. He didn't know about the baby of course, but if I was quick . . . ' I shut my eyes, then opened them again, meeting Mark's honest, painful gaze. 'Yes, you're right. It was a poor, hasty, frightened decision which has haunted me ever since. That's why I've stayed with him this long, really, because I thought I owed it to him. But you tell me, Mark — back then, coming from our sort of background, with Jilly and her illegitimate baby on everyone's lips — what the hell else was I supposed to do?'

Mark was so pale, so shocked, so . . . betrayed. He looked far worse than he did the day Jean left him. 'I had a right to know about Ellie,' he said stubbornly. 'You could have told me later.'

I lifted my hand and let it fall, helpless. 'When? On your first day back at work when you told me Jean was expecting again? When Lydia got meningitis and you were in hospital with her night and day? When you were made redundant and we both borrowed more money than we could afford so we could start up on our own? There was never going to be a right time. I did what I could, Mark. With Ellie and Tori joined at the hip, you almost did bring her up.'

He stumbled to his feet, hurt and betrayal emanating from him like wounds. 'That's not the same and you know it. You're my best friend, Caro. You've always been my best friend. We've talked through good times and bad times. I've trusted you completely and absolutely for two thirds of my life. What's Ellie now, thirty-six? *Thirty-six years* you've deprived me of the right to worry and care about my daughter. I need to walk this off. Don't phone. Don't text. I have to think. I need to just *be* for a while.'

And suddenly there was a space where he wasn't. He was gone and I hadn't expected it. This was worse than awful. It was like a ripped hole in my heart. I curled forward, wrapping my arms around my body, lanced a hundredfold by his pain. Compared to this, my marriage breaking up was an atom of insignificance in the vastness of the universe. Every part of me screamed with loss. This, *this*, was the worst thing in the history of forever.

How was I going to bear the rest of my life if I'd alienated Mark for all time?

* * *

The ringing of my phone interrupted the dreary cycle of fetching stuff from the car and putting it away whilst going over and over my litany of self-recrimination. *Mark*, I thought, my heart leaping. I reached for the phone with shaking fingers.

It wasn't Mark. 'Are you going to be long, Mum?' said Ellie's voice in an only-just-holding-it-together tone. 'Only Dad's been here for half an hour and he's put Duncan's back up *already* by loudly timing every single train and reminding all the kids to be careful when they're running around outside. We've *told* him we're getting new double glazing and that Duncan's father reinforced the wire netting only yesterday, but he's not listening.'

Ellie's housewarming! I shot an aghast look at my ravaged reflection in the mirror. 'Sorry, darling,' I said. 'I'm just finishing up in the office. I'll be there as soon as I can.' I added that Blake was probably tetchy because of his proposed mini-series being turned down yesterday.

'Well, if he wrote something more cheerful and less twisted, he might get accepted more often,' snapped Ellie. 'D'you know, I'm *embarrassed* sometimes to let people know my father wrote whatever it is they're all discussing in the playground. That police thing where the serial killer ripped up his victims' clothing, for instance. That was horrible.'

'Don't tell him that, for goodness sake.'

Ellie muttered something under her breath. 'He'd better stop irritating Duncan, then,' she said aloud. 'I can do without *him* being in a mood too.'

I repeated I'd be there as fast as the legal limit would allow. I repaired my makeup at lightning speed and hoped people would be too involved with eating and drinking and thinking up encouraging things to say about the house to notice how dreadful I looked. As I drove off, it occurred to me with annoyance that Blake would put my blotchy eyes down to him and the revelations of the breakfast table. What a difference a single sentence makes. The truth was I no longer cared enough about him to cry.

★   ★   ★

When I walked into the lounge, Blake nodded at me just as if we hadn't split up irrevocably this morning. I realised with a rueful shock that even that was normal. The marriage had been over for years without my realising it. Why had I stayed? How stupid can one person get?

The house filled with family, neighbours and Ellie and Duncan's friends. The noise level swelled to a cheerful, throbbing crescendo, before dying away again as with the nibbles demolished, the Pimms a memory and the borrowed PTA urn dry, people left to get ready for the concert or their own evening's entertainment. With only the family remaining, we could hear ourselves talk again.

I was sitting on the settee, letting Oliver show me his new iPad. On the other side of the room, Blake seemed to have finished carping about the house and was instead discussing the finer points of free climbing with Duncan's father.

'You can do anything with this, Granny. Anything.'

'I should hope so, the money it cost.'

'Look, I'll show you. Where's Grandad going climbing?'

'I don't know, darling. The Dolomites, wherever they are. He goes there every July.'

Oliver tapped intently on his iPad. 'They're here, Granny. In Italy. Look.' He expanded the map to show all the little wrinkles and contours, with the blue of a lake at the bottom of the screen. He swiped the lake upwards. 'It tells you everything, Granny. That's Lake Garda and the next one is . . . '

Lake Garda.

By chance, there had been a lull in the conversation at the precise moment Oliver spoke. Ellie threw her son a fond glance, clearly congratulating him on entertaining Granny so nicely. Duncan was equally clearly gratified his son was doing something educational rather than explaining at length his current favourite computer game.

Amid the approval I was aware of a brief moment of chill, focused interest from the far side of the room. The conversations started up again. 'You found that just with a name?' I said, as if I hadn't noticed anything. 'You are very clever, Oliver. We'll have to get you doing work experience with Mark as a researcher.'

Lake Garda. Lake Garda. Lake Garda.

'Oh! Where is Mark?' asked Ellie, looking around. 'I asked him especially. I thought he'd come with Tori, but she said he rang telling her he had stuff to do and would be along later. She thought it sounded like an excuse. Is he still uncomfortable about Jean, Mum? She must be mad, don't you think? Going away with a man half her age, just for sex. Poor Mark.'

'He's probably working,' I said, feeling the devastating stab of loss twisting again in my chest. 'And Fernando is only eight years younger than Jean, not half her age at all. Shouldn't you be getting off to the concert? I'll put everything in the dishwasher and hang on for Skye and Rob. You can video Sasha for me.'

Ellie gave a little scream. 'Look at the time! I'm sorry, everyone, but . . . '

The room cleared. There were debates about coats and money-for-the-raffle and who was sharing a lift with whom. Cars drove away. In the distance, a train hurried past. Silence descended.

I remained on the sofa, harnessing the energy to clear up. Oliver's map was still clear and bright in my mind's eye.

The Dolomites, just to the north of Lake Garda.

9

The Dolomites, just to the north of Lake Garda.

I don't know how long I sat there. My mind had gone numb. Blake went to the Dolomites every year. Every year. Even if he spent ninety percent of his time climbing, he couldn't fail to be familiar with the region, with the towns and the lakes. He'd know Lake Garda, where Jilly had lived. He'd know the little town at the top of the lake where Skye's godfather still lived today. Never once, never once in all these years had he mentioned it.

Why?

A shadow darkened the patio door. 'That fence,' said Blake, coming in from the garden wiping rust marks off his hands, 'is not safe at all. The staples have all been ripped from one end. Thieves, I imagine, casing the joint, working out when the house will be empty. I did warn Ellie and Duncan. I told them several times. This whole place is a security breach waiting to happen.'

He was still here. He hadn't gone with everyone else to the concert. A slight tremor went through me. 'Ellie told me Duncan's father had reinforced the fence. He must have missed a bit. It'll be easily fixed. Don't you want to see the concert?' *The Dolomites, just to the north of Lake Garda.*

In the silence, I heard the creak of the old house settling. Somewhere outside a car door banged. The wind found a gap in a window frame and sent a tiny summer draught around my legs.

Blake's gaze rested on me. He said, in a conversational tone, 'Your lack of geographical knowledge has always astounded me, Caro. Jilly was just the same. Useful though, as it turned out.'

My heart thumped. 'Family trait,' I said. 'We had a dreadful geography teacher at school. She put us both off.'

Still he stood there. Looking down at me. 'Funny, isn't it?' he said. 'All these years. I'd begun to think you would never find out.'

Chill swept through me. A memory. Blake's voice, comforting at the time. *She wouldn't have felt anything, falling from height on that sort of terrain.*

Why hadn't I noticed the phrasing? Why had I never brought it to mind since? He'd been to the area. He'd known the road where Jilly had died. Why hadn't he told me? There could only be one answer, one answer, one answer . . .

Peppermint panic rose in my throat. 'What are you saying, Blake? You couldn't have known Jilly was living at the *Castello Acqua di Fonte.*'

Whatever he was going to tell me, I didn't want to know.

'I didn't. I'd never heard of the place until you told me about Skye's godfather. I didn't even know Jilly was in Italy. No, it was simpler than that.

Such a beautiful simplicity, it must have been meant. I thought so at the time.'

I couldn't move, couldn't stop up my ears, couldn't look away.

Blake continued. 'There was a festival on the lake. It's held every year. The other chaps wanted to go. I'd rather have been climbing, but I thought there might be local colour that would come in handy some time. Everything is useful to a writer. So we went and . . . and there was Jilly, in the middle of the crowd, laughing and vibrant, enjoying herself.' His voice went on, clinically dispassionate. 'She was so beautiful, Caro. I'd thought I was over her, but it turned out not. Strange.'

Blake. Blake was why Jilly had run away. Blake was the stalker. He'd done that trick of getting an idea in his head and then not letting go. Jilly had probably just been being friendly and not even realised he had fallen for her until it was too late. Oh God.

'She said she was with a group. I thought she meant on holiday, not living there. I didn't want to sit at that big table with her friends. I wanted her to myself. I said I was getting local colour and asked if she wanted to walk around with me so we could have a catch-up. She said she'd better not, it would look rude. Then there was a burst of noise from her table with children shouting and wailing and she suddenly changed her mind and said okay, just a short walk then. I steered her away from the festival, towards the outskirts where it was quieter. I told her I'd missed her. I wanted to know why she left, what she'd been doing, why she hadn't contacted me. I wanted to know everything. It was as if I was starving. I wanted to drink her in.'

I sat frozen, unable to believe what I was hearing. In another burst of sickening memory, I remembered the only drama of his I'd ever watched all the way through. The one about obsession. The one about obsession and the stalker and the woman he idolised.

It's only dancing, Caro.

Oh God. Oh God. Oh God.

Blake continued, almost reminiscently now. 'Jilly said she'd felt stifled in England and had had to get away. She said she hadn't told me because she hadn't thought we were in a serious relationship. She'd thought we were just friends, no more than that, sorry if she'd misunderstood. She said she was nowhere near ready to go back home yet. She liked travelling. She liked new experiences. She liked being a rolling stone and said there was far too much of the rest of the world to see before she returned. Then she said it had been nice to chat and started walking up the road.' His voice hardened. 'Walking away from me. Again.'

No, don't tell me. Please don't tell me. It's not true.

'I was quite calm. I'd brought her in this direction because I'd left my car here. I thought we might sit in it to talk if there was nowhere else. As she walked away, she passed it by the side of the road.'

Don't tell me!

Blake smiled as if to share with me how beautifully everything had fitted. 'It was serendipity, you see? I'd already told the others I'd probably not hang around until the evening like them, that I'd see them back at the hotel. I started the car, drove around the first long bend and there she was, ahead of me. It was so easy. Just as if it was meant. I remember she was wearing a dress the colour of summer, all oranges and reds. It belled out as she flew over the edge. She sailed, Caro, sailed out and down the hillside. But I didn't see, because I was already driving on, back to the climbing ridge.'

I gripped the edge of the coffee table, sick abhorrence overwhelming me. My Jilly. My darling, lovely Jilly. I could see the road in my mind's eye. I could feel the dry heat in my throat. It was as if I'd lost her all over again.

'I thought that would be an end to it,' said the man whose bed I'd shared for thirty-seven years, 'but I discovered I was still angry with her. Those shoes I bought her. I found them in your wardrobe and thought she'd left them behind so they wouldn't get spoilt, but then you said she'd *given* them to you. Given! I took that out on Astrid after you left. I had to give her extra money. Did I say how furious I was with you for getting rid of the au pairs, by the way? They were so convenient, Caro, and I made sure the children were never neglected. I enjoyed making sure of it, if we're being honest. But no, you interfered. I had to take a room in town after that.'

I was rigid with revulsion. I wanted to blank out the thin stream of hatred coming from his mouth. I wanted to slam a thousand decibels of Queen into the car CD player and hurtle back to the office. I wanted bright lights and Camden bustle and noise and colour and normality. I wanted to phone Mark and hear his sane, familiar voice and hold myself against the warmth of his t-shirt. But Mark was gone. I'd lost his trust. Besides, I couldn't move, couldn't even retch. I was one long scream, trapped in stone.

Blake glanced at the clock, looked out at the garden, put his hand on the latch of the patio door. 'Come on, Caro, the seven-fifteen is due. You do see I can't let you tell anyone, don't you?'

I must have made some sort of noise because he shook his head in faint amusement.

'I'm afraid, even if you promise to keep quiet, I won't believe you. You talk too much, always have. The only reason I ever put up with it was because of Skye.' He smiled at me, his eyes kind and regretful and quite, quite mad. A genuine laugh broke from him. 'Why, I didn't even know Jilly had had our baby until you told me. I'd been looking for you, you know, that week, to judge by your behaviour whether she'd been found and whether anyone had told you. When I saw you crying, I was sure of it. Then you opened your mouth and gave me this great gift. Plus the sting in the tail that made me angry with Jilly all over again. She knew I wanted a family, she knew I had it all mapped out. And yet she pretended she hadn't realised I was serious. She made you, and only you, Skye's guardian in perpetuity. I've had to let so many things go by, Caro, simply because you could have taken Skye away from me.'

The breeze against my legs was stronger. Ellie and Duncan must have left the front door open. If I could just move, I could get out to the street and run and run and run.

Blake glanced at the clock again. 'Time to go, Caro. Get up off the sofa, there's a good girl. Poor Ellie, how many times have I warned her that fence isn't safe? They won't be able to live here now, not after this. It would give them nightmares. They'll have to move again. They'll never get back what they paid for the house. Such a stupid choice. I did tell them.'

In thirty-seven years of marriage, I

had never once been afraid of Blake. I was now. He crossed the room and grasped my wrist. I felt his insane, focused strength as he hauled me to my feet.

'No,' I said, leaning away from him. I might as well have tried to resist the winch drive of a steel hawser or the power of the Flying Scotsman in full steam.

Blake's grip tightened as he pulled me towards the patio door. 'It won't hurt, Caro. You'll just trip down the bank and on to the rails. Easy to explain in those shoes. You won't feel a thing, I promise.'

'No,' I said, grabbing desperately at the wing of an armchair as I passed and feeling it thump into my calf as it toppled backwards. I lurched. He heaved me upright. 'No, Blake!'

He bent to hoist me up. 'The word you are looking for is 'yes'.'

'You heard, Blake. Let go of Caro now,' ground out a voice behind me.

Gladness flooded me, glorious, with choirs of angels ascending. My first thought — far out in front, way beyond any sense of my own danger — was that Mark had come to Ellie's housewarming after all. Did that mean he'd forgiven me? Was there still hope?

I twisted my head — and caught my breath. He stood in the doorway, as invincible as if carved in silvered oak, tough and ready to fight like an avenging god. Ready to fight Blake for *me*. Skye had arrived too and was a step behind him. Their profiles against the stark white of the walls looked identical, but where Mark's expression was deadly, Skye was drained of colour.

'Dad?' said Skye said in disbelief.

'Skye!' Blake's grip faltered. His face reflected Skye's horror.

In the distance we heard the whistle of the train. I automatically glanced at the clock. When I looked back, my wrist was free, the patio door was ajar and Blake was no longer there. Mark took two long strides across the room, turning my face to his chest and holding me close as we heard the screech of metal brakes on metal rails.

10

'He didn't stand a chance,' said the policeman, drawing a line under his notes. 'That'll be the ambulance now. I'll tell them where to go.'

There was the sound of men's voices, heavy boots. I stood up, uncertain of my role.

'Don't go out there, Mum,' said Skye urgently.

'I'm not going to.' I closed the patio curtains with a shudder. My gaze fell on the clock again. Sasha would just be singing now. Incredible what a short space of time had passed.

Skye's voice cracked, 'Dad, though. I just can't believe it. We . . . we heard everything. Was it true?'

I looked at my boy, Jilly's boy. He and Rob sat close to each other for comfort on the settee, next to where I'd just got up. Mark was perched on the arm. He'd rested a protective hand on my shoulder all the time the police had been here. For all his thirty-eight years, Skye looked as blank and uncomprehending as he'd been on that long ago day in Alessandro's study.

'Yes, it was true,' I said. 'Blake was obsessed with Jilly. You know how he is, sometimes. She got scared and went abroad. She thought he'd calm down after a few years and she could come back. In his eyes, her leaving was a rejection. When he accidentally met her again and she told him it had never been serious, I think it must have turned him a bit mad. He killed her, more or less on the spur of the moment. He was the hit and run driver. Then he found out about you and transferred all the original affection he'd had for Jilly to you. He did sincerely love you, Skye.'

And that, of course, was the real reason he'd thrown himself in front of the train. He couldn't live with the horror on Skye's face. I wasn't going to tell Skye and Rob that though. Too much guilt. Let them think it was the fear of discovery.

So much explained. The way the Biba shoes he'd given Jilly had been on the au pair one day and in shreds in the dustbin the next. The way he'd gone ballistic when I'd sent a family photo to Alessandro one year instead of an updated picture of Skye alone. He must have been alarmed in case Alessandro innocently identified him as a regular to the town — or worse, in case he was recognised as a man Jilly was seen talking to on the day she died.

'I feel sick,' said Skye, his voice shaking. 'I wish he hadn't been my father. I feel unclean.'

Rob made a distressed sound and held him closer.

'He wasn't your father,' I said crisply, moving across the room. This at least I could do something about. I'd have preferred a better time, but this was urgent. 'Listen to me, Skye. He'd convinced himself he was, but he wasn't.'

'Mum, do you know that for sure?' There was desperate hope in Skye's eyes. Beside him, Rob's hand was clenched on his.

'Yes,' I said, putting all the conviction I could muster into my voice. 'Yes, I know it for certain. I know Jilly didn't run away because she was pregnant. That happened later, after she'd gone. She ran because she was scared. Scared of Blake. She left the day after he went on holiday. She was so frightened of his obsession she went on an unscheduled documentary shoot with Mark, just to get away. I wish she'd told me to begin with. I wish she'd told me in the letters she wrote and never posted. I would never have let Blake anywhere near you if I'd known he was the reason she left.' I gave a half laugh. 'I could have done with knowing who your real father was too.'

Except, in a roundabout way, she'd told me that as well, hadn't she? What had she written?

There are reasons why I'm not saying

who Skye's father is. Trust me, though, he has the best of genes. Skye will grow up a brilliant boy who'll look after me beautifully in my old age.

Yes. Yes, it had to be. People often remarked on the likeness between Skye and Ellie, always putting it down to me and Jilly being cousins. I'd thought exactly the same myself for years. Blake must have secretly preened, the likeness reinforcing his belief that the children had the same father.

Facing them all now, my conviction grew. In the split second this evening when I'd turned to see Mark bursting through the door with Skye just behind him, I'd realised my children *did* have the same father. But it wasn't Blake. Whatever Jilly might have got up to during her crazy, running-scared fortnight in New York, my money was on that cruise liner back from the States.

'Skye,' I said, hunkering down in front of him and taking his free hand. 'I've always known your father wasn't Blake. But I've only just now, just this minute actually, worked out who it really is.'

There was a stirring of interest in the room. 'Who?' asked Skye. 'How can you suddenly know now?'

I swallowed and took Mark's hand as well. 'Because I do know Jilly. I knew her all along. I'm pretty sure I'm right. The dates fit. The circumstances fit.'

I brought their hands together, both my men. 'Mark, I'm sorry, you need to prepare yourself for another shock. I seem to have brought up your son as well as your daughter. Skye, love, meet your dad.'

* * *

'Me?' said Mark, still lost for words twenty minutes later. 'Me?'

We were back on the sofa. The police had gone. Ellie and the rest had been texted, frantic calls had been exchanged and they were due back from the concert within the next half hour. Rob and Skye were in the kitchen. Rob had declared that no matter the alarms and tragedies of the day, people would need to be fed and Skye needed to be doing something, so he'd borne him off for a bit of intensive KP. I leant against Mark, revelling in his warmth, the closeness of his body filling years of aching need.

'It adds up, Mark,' I said. 'Think about it. Your cruise documentary date *does* fit with Skye's birthday. *You* are the reason Jilly wouldn't say who the father was, quite apart from being worried about Blake and what he might do.' I gripped Mark's hand, swallowing a moment of nausea that I had been married for nearly forty years to my cousin's killer. I was going to have to work hard not to let that become a nightmare. I needed to focus on being angry instead. Angry that he'd robbed me of a normal, loving life. So many wasted, hijacked years when Mark and I could have . . .

Mark rubbed his face. 'I've seen the likeness so many times and not realised.

Family expressions, I thought. I never even dreamt the link might have been me.'

I was only dancing, Caro, the same as I think you'd like to do, except you're a better person than me.

Yes, Jilly had told me. She'd seen my feelings for Mark back when I believed we were just friends. Decades, the two of us had lost, by being honourable and doing the right thing. It was time to change that, right now.

I took a deep breath. 'The point is, Mark, Jilly may have been only dancing, back then on the cruise ship, but I wasn't, the night in my flat. It was real. I've loved you as long as I've known you. This is the first time I've been able to do anything about it.'

His arm came around my shoulders, firm and sure. I looked up at him.

'I love you,' I repeated. 'I nearly died when I hurt you so badly you walked out of the office this morning. Is it too late?'

His eyes were full of warmth and

promise and regret that it had taken both of us this long. 'Come off it, Caro, we aren't even sixty yet. Bags of time.' He pulled me closer. 'I've loved you for years. I should have done this that morning I woke up next to you.' He bent his head until his lips brushed mine, paused for a final eternity of no-going-back, then we moved seamlessly into a future of our own choosing as he kissed me and I kissed him and mountains moved and choirs of angels ascended all over again and in the solid centre of whirling gold was Mark and me, together.

SECRETS OF MELLIN COVE

Rena George

After Wenna discovers a shocking family secret, she flies to the comfort of her beloved Cornish moors. What can she do? If she reveals the terrible truth, her family will be ruined. If she does nothing, she could be condemning the crew of a sailing ship to death. Perhaps she should confide in the tall stranger who rides past her every day, always casting an interested glance in her direction. But would he understand, or would he go straight to the authorities? No, she couldn't trust a stranger . . . or could she?

RUNAWAY LOVE

Fay Wentworth

When Emma flees to Leigh Manor to escape the pain of a broken romance, she finds that life there as a secretary to Alex Baron is not as simple as she anticipated. An unfortunate encounter between herself, Alex and a bull heralds the start of a fiery relationship. And what is the mystery behind the charming façade of Blake, Alex's assistant? As Emma's new job gets off to a rocky start, she soon finds herself wondering who she can trust — and whether coming to Leigh Manor was a good idea . . .

GIFT OF THE NILE

Heidi Sullivan

Amber Davis has always loved hearing about her father's archaeological excavations, and is thrilled when she is finally allowed to accompany the professor on an expedition. As she begins her Egyptian adventure, she meets expatriates Lachlan and his son James. Amber is drawn to the artistic and bohemian James, but is concerned about the lecherous eye of his father. When things begin to go very wrong during the trip, can Amber keep her head . . . and her heart?

TRUSTING A STRANGER

Sarah Purdue

Clara Radley's life is all about her studies until she is woken in the night by hammering on her front door. Into her world steps handsome US Special Agent Jack Henry, who tells her that her life is in danger and his job is to protect her. Henry has been sent by her biological father — a US Army General who Clara has never even met. How can she trust this stranger? But what choice does she have?